Raising Sir Gallant

written by Mary Bustamante

illustrated by Mary Flock Lempa

For a more interactive experience,
this story can be enjoyed in conjunction with the

Sir Gallant Castle Kit

Enclosed in a hinged wooden castle, the Sir Gallant Castle Kit brings Gallant's knight adventure to life with a corresponding Workbook, fifteen Banners (chapter award ribbons), two story-related Gifts and three hand-made and/or hand-assembled high-quality story-related Crafts.* One final special surprise awaits those fearless young adventurers who dare to complete all the lessons and crafts. As a reward for finishing their course, they are permitted to break open the wax seal and read the Secret Knight Letter. It is then that they will find their quest is just beginning...

* The Sir Gallant Castle Kit arrives fully stocked for one inquisitive and resolute knight-in-training. Additional Workbooks, Banners, Gifts, Crafts and Secret Knight Letters are available for purchase at SirGallant.com for pleading siblings, homeschool groups and classroom applications.

The Raising Sir Gallant Storybook is available at SirGallant.com.

Raising Sir Gallant

The lessons that transformed
a young farm boy into a knight.

By Mary Bustamante

Illustrated by Mary Flock Lempa

Biblical quotes are taken from the Douay-Rheims translation,
1899 American Edition; and/or the Latin Vulgate, 400 AD

Cover art and Illustrations by Mary Flock Lempa
Interior design and layout by Michelle M. White
The Broadsheet™ font used throughout this story was created by
Brian Willson. His unique collection of type designs can be found at
Oldfonts.com

ISBN 978-1-7337599-8-4

Second edition printed by Kindle Direct Publishing.

BRISTOL & THORNBURY, LLC

In Thanksgiving to the Lord God,
for the countless boys who will
mature into great men;
strengthened by His Grace,
moved by His Wisdom and
guided by His Word.

Table of Contents

Acknowledgments

Whether the *Raising Sir Gallant* project becomes a wildly popular classic or just remains a personal favorite, I am most grateful that the Lord placed a love for writing in my heart and inspired me to tell the story of young Gallant.

I thank the Lord also for wonderful parents who taught me the lessons needed to navigate this world: thank you, Cecelia and Anthony†, for showing me what it means to live well. The rest of my family contributed in ways known and unknown to them. Thank you all.

My sincerest appreciation to all those who encouraged my writing and helped by reviewing my story as it progressed: teachers, family, friends and colleagues, especially my parents and my sister and brother, Mrs. Shipp and Sr. Christen, Bob†, Ann Marie, Lisa, Bruce, Ed, Ron, David, Bill, Theresa, Amy, Merv, Todd, Maday, Dave, Cindy, Beth, Chris, Susan, Mary, Lori, Barb, Christine, Henry, Bob & Diane, Glenn, my Illustrator, Mary and my Editor, Cynthia. I also learned a great deal from my writing group: Jennifer, Linda, Dan and Randy; thank you all. The first edition leather-bound hardcover book would not have come together so beautifully without the design assistance provided by Michelle at MMWBooks.com and the careful guidance by Steve at BindTech-Kingsport Bindery.

Preface

If your father was a knight in England 650 years ago, your training to follow in his footsteps would have begun early in your life. When you turned seven, you would have been sent to a castle and given the title: page. For years, you would clean the armor of knights and run their errands without question and without complaining. If you performed your service well, you would move on to the role of squire when you turned fourteen.

A hundred other boys would have jumped at the chance to be where you would be, handing a knight his sword just before he leapt into battle; or guarding him in the evening as he slept. If you finished your full course of study with honor, you would be promoted to a knight when you turned twenty-one. As part of this elite class of men, you would be most admired for your honesty. Your code of honor would require you to assist those in need, especially the poor, widows and orphans. Even though you had the training and the strength to fight, you would only resort to battle when reasoned negotiation failed or when someone's life was in immediate danger.

Do you have what it takes to be a knight?

At the end of each chapter, you will find a list of word definitions called the **Word Helper**. The words included in the list are printed in **boldface** in the story. Place a bookmark at the *next* **Word Helper** before you begin each chapter. Then, if you need a definition, you can easily flip to the list and then back to your place in the story. If you don't know a word, look it up! Did you know? It's what a knight would do.

CHAPTER ONE

Strange Sounds in the Forest

Bristol, England
In the year 1517

Gallant was sore and covered with twigs. He had been crawling about in the woods since daybreak and he was hungry. The fig jam on his barley bread quieted his growling stomach, but now his snack was gone and his brief rest was over. He shook the last tart drops of cider onto his outstretched tongue and pulled the rope of his flask over his head and shoulder, swinging the leather bottle behind his back. With a contented sigh, he reached for the smooth stick at his feet. A week earlier he had whittled off the smaller branches and stretched a woolen string from one end to the other, a span one-half again longer than his arm. He stood silently behind the broad trunk of an enormous oak tree and faced the gentle breeze, squinting as he surveyed the forest in the mid-day sun.

Within minutes, he spied a plump beige rabbit in the distance. Utilizing the cover of thick **foliage**, Gallant shuffled toward his target in short, unevenly-timed steps. If the young boy had learned the technique properly, the rabbit would hear only the rustling a squirrel would make as it scurried to collect its buried acorns. Gallant paused where the shrubbery ended. He watched the rabbit hop to a fresh bloom of tender shoots growing in a sunny patch between trees. The hunter-in-training knew he had to hurry. Now that the rabbit had left the shade for an open field, it would eat as much as it could as fast as it could, before rushing back to the safety of its nest.

Gallant examined the patch of tall softly-swaying grass before him. Noisy squirrel sounds wouldn't do. He was now a quiet, slow-moving deer, whose long tapered legs stepped nimbly through the dense thicket. The rabbit was still munching contentedly, undisturbed by the sounds of the forest.

Springtime saw the mournful browns of the winter woods gradually overcome by the bright shades of green and the emerging **palette** of color splashed high and low. Gallant wore his olive-colored long-sleeve shirt and tunic and his tan pants, which helped him to blend in with tree trunks and low-hanging branches. He kept to the shadows whenever possible; and early that day he had smeared cooled ash on his cheeks and forehead as a way to darken his light face, something he learned by watching his father. But he wasn't only worried about being seen and heard; he also had to consider the keen sense of smell that alerted wild animals to their predators.

Already there was so much to consider, but not seven days past, Gallant's father had increased the difficulty of the hunting game. "Carry a tree branch with you," he instructed, "pretend it is your bow and arrow."

Gallant got within twenty paces of his **prey** without being discovered. *So far so good*, he thought to himself. *Only three paces more and I will be the closest I have ever been.* Crouched low behind a thick bush, he peered through leafy branches at the rabbit nibbling on wild **fennel**. He cradled his branch in the elbow crook of one arm and slowly reached forward with the other. Just as he set his hand down, a dry branch snapped under his palm. The rabbit bolted upright onto its hind legs. Its large ears swiveled about and then froze in the direction of Gallant.

The boy held his breath. *You mustn't hear me,* he thought. *Not now...not when I'm this close!* Five seconds passed. Gallant stayed motionless. Ten seconds. The rabbit twitched its whiskers and dipped back to its snack of yellow flower petals. Gallant slowly exhaled. He leaned forward and resumed his crawl.

At that moment, a clamor echoed through the trees and the rabbit dashed out of sight. The noises sounded like metal striking metal—*but how could that be? I'm in the middle of a forest!* Gallant remained where he was, hidden by the bush, and waited. The clashing grew louder and now it was accompanied by heavy, labored breathing.

"Aaarrrghhh. Uhhhhhh." Suddenly, two men came into view. "Aaaaaaahhhh! Arggghh!"

They were **obscured** from Gallant's full view, but now he could see they were fighting with long silver swords. Streaks of light flashed from the blades as the sharp edges caught the sunlight. The fierce clanging of the metal increased as the men struck with greater force.

Gallant's heart began to race. *What if one of the men was injured—or killed?* Just when the boy decided to run for help, one of the fighters fell so near that the thud shook the ground under Gallant. The man on the ground groaned and turned his head to reach for the sword he had dropped. Gallant gasped: *Oh no! It's Father!* A stranger pointed his blade at Gallant's father as he lay on the ground, moaning.

"On your feet, you **rascal**!" the victor shouted gruffly.

Without thinking, Gallant leapt out from behind the bush and ran to the battle, still clutching his stick. He waved the piece of wood and shouted at the stranger: "Get back! Stay away from my father!"

Now that Gallant was out in the open, he realized that the stranger towered over him. *I can't fight him, he's twice my size. And that sword! It's as tall as I am!* Gallant suddenly felt dizzy. His knees wobbled, and he backed up a step. Another minute and he might have fainted; but just then, the man lowered his sword and stepped back. He looked closely at the boy before him, and said calmly, "You've got your father's dark hair and your mother's blue eyes. Hmmm. You're too old to be Timothy. You must be Gallant."

The swordsman turned to Gallant's father. "William, this is a brave lad. You've taught him well. How old is he? Eight?"

Gallant was stunned that the man with the sword was suddenly speaking in a friendly tone. *How does he know my name? And why is he smiling at me?* The boy bent down to help his father to his feet, careful not to lose his grip on his wooden stick.

William responded proudly, in between breaths. "He's nine, ahhh, but as you see, he has the **pluck** of a wild **boar**!" Standing at his father's side, Gallant began to recover. He studied the stranger and then looked back at his father. His father wasn't afraid and neither man was interested in sword-fighting anymore. *Were they just playing?*

William was still breathing heavily as he brushed the dirt and leaves from his light-colored woolen shirt. He wore snug pants and ankle-high leather boots. He **gestured** toward the stranger and smiled. "Gallant," his father said in between breaths, "Don't be afraid, ah, whew, Francis is a friend from my youth. I became a farmer and he, well, he became a knight." Gallant's eyes grew wide and he turned with amazement to the stranger. William took a deep breath and made a formal introduction: "Sir Francis, I present my son Gallant." And to his son, he said: "Gallant, this is Sir Francis."

"I regret I startled you." Sir Francis bowed to Gallant deeply, pausing momentarily when his head was low and within striking distance of Gallant's stick. It was the kind of bow ordinarily reserved for royalty.

Gallant should have bowed in return, just as his father had taught him, but he was too stunned to move. *I've always wanted to meet a knight. Here I am, in the middle of a forest, face to face with a real, live knight!*

The shock of what happened was wearing off, but now the boy was feeling embarrassed. *Did I really challenge a knight with a tree branch?* He examined Sir Francis carefully. This knight wasn't anything like Gallant had expected. He wore linen traveling clothes, a long olive-colored tunic, and russet pants, not armor. A thick shock of blond hair fell over a forehead that was tan from the sun and glistening with perspiration. Sir Francis bore a leather **satchel** swung sideways across his chest and his sword scabbard was anchored to a wide leather belt. His boots had leather strips crisscrossed from his feet up to his knees. Gallant would have assumed he were just an ordinary traveler, were it not for the sword he carried.

Sir Francis turned his attention to Gallant. "When you charged from the brush, you faced me completely, squared off, like this. You see?" Sir Francis turned so he was directly facing Gallant. "But unless you need both hands on the sword, you ought to blade your body so it is less of a target for your opponent." Sir Francis positioned himself sideways and extended his sword out toward Gallant to demonstrate. "Try it," he said.

Gallant glanced at his father, who nodded his encouragement, so Gallant followed Sir Francis' example and held his branch out toward the knight.

"Good. Now bend your knees so you can move quickly," Sir Francis continued. "Watch my sword, not my face."

Sir Francis waved the sword toward Gallant and allowed him to strike it several times with his branch. He moved in a circle around Gallant, showing the boy how to move his feet without tripping over them. "Never cross your feet as you move," Sir Francis instructed. "You're sure to lose your balance, or worse, trip and fall into your opponent's sword."

Gallant tried to sidestep the way Sir Francis did. It was hard to do and within a few seconds, he caught his toe on a protruding rock and fell sideways to the ground. He scuffled back to his feet.

"That's enough for your first lesson." Sir Francis sheathed his sword. "I see you've got instincts like your father. Someday, no doubt, you will have his strength."

William nudged Sir Francis, "So now what do you say, old friend?"

Sir Francis responded, "I concede, William. A farmer *is* as strong as a knight."

"Ah, yes," William responded, "but clearly your skill was superior. You could have split me in two."

Sir Francis laughed. "You must admit it's harder than it looks from the fairground stands."

"Indeed."

Gallant was still a little dazed, but now that the shock had passed, he started to feel nervous. He had heard a true knight could read hearts as though they were pages of a book. He had never expected to meet a knight, and now he wasn't sure how to keep the secret in his heart hidden from Sir Francis. He decided to avoid eye contact with him until Sir Francis left their company.

Gallant's father turned his attention to the boy. "How was your hunt, son?"

"I was within twenty paces of a rabbit, father."

"You're getting better!" William turned to Sir Francis. "The boy's got an eye for the slightest movement in the forest. He spotted the two hares we will enjoy for supper tonight!"

Gallant stared at the ground, hoping to avoid further discussion. Sir Francis would be on his way soon, Gallant reasoned. *Surely a knight has important business to do, meeting with the king and his nobles.* But instead of bidding William farewell, Sir Francis clapped him on the back.

"Perhaps there will be enough to share," Sir Francis said boldly. "I have a proposal to make, but it will require a good meal and some ale. Now then, show me to your home, won't you?"

Gallant held his breath as he waited to see how his father would respond.

"Splendid," William said. He sounded eager. "This way, then." He turned and led the way through the forest.

Oh, no! Gallant dragged his stick in the dirt and followed several steps behind the two men, feeling uneasy at the prospect of spending too much time with someone who could read his heart. When they reached a meadow near the road, Sir Francis retrieved his horse, which he left grazing where he first encountered Gallant's father. The muscular, **chestnut**-colored horse had an arched neck, a neatly trimmed dark mane, and a thick, blunt tail.

Sir Francis unfastened the belt at his waist and wrapped it around the sheathed sword, then tied it just below the saddle, along the flank of the horse. The animal pawed the ground with a front hoof.

"Yes, Donato. A cool drink would do us both some good!" Sir Francis said as he patted the horse's neck. William handed Sir Francis the sword he had been using, and he strapped it alongside the other. Once the knight's gear was secure, William picked up a bulging **burlap** sack lying on the ground nearby and slung it over his back. He normally carried the sack on the days he walked across their property and trimmed back the fruit trees or repaired the fences, but he had been unexpectedly interrupted in the middle of this work to **spar** with his friend.

Sir Francis gathered the reins and scratched the cheek of his horse as he walked; William on one side and his majestic animal on the other, Gallant straggling behind. Together they followed the road leading to William's home, a path little more than two worn strips where wagon wheels had cut through the wildflowers. Were it not for his worry, Gallant would have continued his hunting game, scanning the trees above for the squirrels he knew were quietly watching them pass. But Gallant was lost in his thoughts, barely aware of the squirrels or the conversation.

"Just before I fell," William was saying, "you could have taken my leg at the knee with that wide sweep. How might I have deflected it?"

Sir Francis thought a moment. "Hmm. It's tough to recover once exposed in that way, unless you planned it, of course. In the tournaments, an open leg is often a ploy to get the opponent off-balance. Had you known that trick, you might have ended the battle with one well-timed thrust!"

The two men bantered about the fineries of swordplay until they were close enough to see the trail of smoke rising from Gallant's home. The nearer they came to the house, the farther Gallant fell behind, swatting at the brush with his stick and mumbling **reprimands** to himself.

"Keep up lad!" William called back to him.

Gallant quickened his pace. *If only I had done the right thing last year, I could be telling Sir Francis the story, instead of trying to hide it from him.*

Think About This

1. Gallant always wanted to meet a real knight. When he finally did, what was the one thing that worried him?

2. Gallant thought knights could read hearts. Do you think this is really possible? Or could it be knights learn how good men act and how bad men act and simply read their actions?

3. It takes a lot of energy to keep a secret that you know should be told. What do you think Gallant should do?

Gallant (sounds like **gail**-ent): a proper noun, the name of our main character; the adjective gallant means brave, valiant

foliage (sounds like **fole**-ee-ig): a noun, the leaves of a plant

palette (sounds like **pal**-it): a noun, a variety of colors

prey (sounds like **pray**): a noun, an animal being hunted

fennel (sounds like **fen**-ell): a noun, a plant similar to parsley

obscured (sounds like ub-**skuur**-d): an adverb, hard to see, hidden from full view

rascal (sounds like **rass**-gull): a noun, a person who is mischievous

pluck (sounds like **pluck**): a noun, bravery

boar (sounds like **bore**): a noun, an aggressive, wild pig

gestured (sounds like **jest**-yer-d): a verb, a movement of the hand toward something

russet (sounds like **russ**-set): a noun, a coarse reddish-brown color

satchel (sounds like **sat**-chill): a noun, a cloth bag

scuffled (sounds like **skuff**-ld): a verb, to scrape feet while moving

concede (sounds like kahn-**seed**): a verb, to acknowledge or submit, sometimes reluctantly, to another person or point of view

chestnut (sounds like **chess**-nutt): a noun, a brown-colored edible nut

burlap (sounds like **burr**-lap): a noun, rough fabric made from plant material

spar (sounds like **spar**): a verb, to fight or to pretend to fight

reprimands (sounds like **rep**-rim-mandz): a noun, a series of corrections, scolding

If you have the Sir Gallant Castle Kit, go to your Workbook now and complete the first lesson, called Banner 1.

CHAPTER TWO

ñiding a ñeart Inside a ñome

William, Sir Francis, and Gallant left the dense forest and approached a country home nestled in a clearing near a sloping hill. When Sir Francis saw the front arch of the building and the livestock grazing behind a sturdy fence, he spoke with admiration, "Well, it is no surprise to me that you have built such a handsome homestead."

William placed his hand on his son's head. "I had help," he said proudly. "He'll be quite a carpenter someday."

Sir Francis turned to the young boy with genuine interest. "Tell me about it," he said.

Gallant worried about talking to Sir Francis. *Maybe this is how he does it. Maybe getting me to talk is how he reads my heart.* He didn't answer right away, and his father looked over at him sternly. It was rude not to answer an adult, and Gallant knew his father was not pleased with the delay. He took a deep breath and began to tell the tale. It was just last year they had finished the project, and he remembered it well.

"Father and some men from the village dug holes two and a half **fathoms** apart and put large wooden beams into the ground, there," Gallant said, motioning toward the front of the house. As they approached, Gallant pointed to the two corners of the structure where the beams emerged from the ground. "The top of each shaft was curved, you see? The two ends bent toward each other." Gallant set down his stick and cupped his hands together, making a rounded tent-shape with his fingers to show Sir Francis.

Sir Francis pressed him further. "But what kept them from falling in toward each other?" he asked.

Gallant didn't see Sir Francis wink at William. The knight already knew how houses were constructed, but he was testing Gallant, noting carefully how Gallant spoke and whether or not he retained the information he had learned the prior year when he helped the builders.

"A brace was added, from one to the other," Gallant stepped forward and gestured toward an area above the front door. "Here. Just above the door. Once the structure was braced, the beams were roped and crossed at the top like an X."

Sir Francis nodded. "Go on."

"Several more shafts were buried in the ground the same way down the entire length of the home. After the **horizontal** braces were in place for each pair, they laid a log across the top, where the beams came together in the X, running one end to the other. They added support timbers to all four sides and then we filled in the walls with a mixture of clay, straw, and twig," Gallant explained.

"So," responded Sir Francis, "as long as you keep the roof patched, I'll bet the woven **reeds** deflect the rain and snow."

"Yes, sir. It's my job to watch for leaks." Gallant was genuinely excited to have an opportunity to explain his efforts to an adult. Most children were taught not to speak to adults or visitors except for short greetings and pleasantries.

Now Gallant was eager to finish the story. "There's one door, and two glass windows. We lower wooden covers down over the windows at night and in harsh weather."

"Glass windows," Sir Francis said, marveling at the details. "Those aren't often seen in a village house. I'm pleased for you."

William pointed to the far side of the house. "Tell him about the back area, Gallant."

"It's fenced, there, behind the house, and the animals are brought inside the pen for the evening." Gallant continued. "Father built a roof to cover the area closest to the house, so the sheep and goats can get out of the rain on the bad days; and we constructed a couple stalls to hold the animals for milking. With our chicken coop we have a brood of hens that provide fresh eggs every morning."

William nodded toward another building about thirty steps from the house. "That's our stable," he said. "We added a storeroom a few months ago, and Catherine keeps a garden on the other side of it. By the grace of God, the well was here when we arrived. It's cool, deep and untainted. I'm told this land was once owned by Giovanni Caboto."

"The explorer?" Sir Francis raised his brow, "Ah, if only wells could tell. What stories we might hear!"

Sir Francis led his horse to the water trough near the well, removed the bridle from its head and waited as it drank. When the knight began to walk again toward the farmhouse with William and Gallant, the horse followed.

They neared the front door, Sir Francis nodding his approval at the homestead. A neat stack of firewood occupied the space on one side of the door, a large wooden barrel on the other. The markings on the barrel indicated it had once carried Bordeaux wine from France, but now it lay on its side, the top half removed. Wood blocks kept it from rolling so it could be used as a bathtub, carried into the house on frigid days and left outside in the sun during the summer. Sir Francis stopped walking and turned to William. "Does Gallant know his letters?"

"Thanks to Catherine, he can read and write," William answered. Then he leaned into Sir Francis and added, whispering, "—though he rushes, and his printing could be neater."

Gallant was amazed he was standing so near a knight; and although he was still concerned his secret would be revealed, his curiosity was growing. *When was Sir Francis knighted? Who gave him his sword? How many battles had he fought? Had he ever been injured?*

The smoke from inside the home seeped through several openings in the roof and disappeared in wisps above the house. Gallant's mother pushed open the door and greeted them with a smile. The scent of rabbit stew filled the air. By now it was mid-afternoon. She must have been watching for them.

"Welcome, welcome," she said cheerily. William clutched his wife's hand in a sweet greeting and held the door for her to return inside. He then motioned to Sir Francis to enter, with he and Gallant following the knight through the doorway.

"You'll stay for a hot meal and a night's good rest," William said. It was an invitation, but the way Gallant's father said it, it sounded more like an order. Sir Francis nodded his eager acceptance.

Gallant's little sister ran to their father. "Papa!" The long sleeves of her loose pale blue dress were turned back at the wrist and the skirt skimmed the floor. A larger size dress or shirt for the little ones meant they could continue wearing the item as they grew. Most farm folk only had one set of outer wool clothing, which they wore until the patching of bare or torn areas was no longer effective to hold the heat in winter. For the cold weather days, men wore sheepskin jackets or cloaks, and women wore capes.

Each member of the family also had two sets of linen underclothing, used for both working and sleeping. One set they wore, while the other was being washed. The underclothing was cleaned more often than the outer; scrubbed with soap, then soaked in lavender water and hung to dry outside, or near the fire during bad weather. Gallant and his siblings were each blessed with extra shirts and dresses, because of the family's success in the wool trade.

"This is Margaret," William announced proudly, stroking his daughter's cheek. "She's five, but sometimes she thinks she is in charge of the household." Margaret giggled and hugged his leg. William scooped her up and held her as he introduced a small boy hidden behind the gathers of his mother's long gray skirt. "And that young man playing hide-and-seek is Timothy. He just turned three." The boy wore an off-white shirt tucked into tan breeches that were tied with fabric strips at the knee. He was dressed in long cream-colored wool socks that covered his knees. His small leather slippers buttoned on the side. William laughed as he explained, "Timothy collects every rock he can carry. I expect he will be a great stone cutter one day."

Sir Francis greeted each child and then reached in the satchel he carried and pulled out candied ginger pieces, one for Margaret and one for Timothy. He didn't give one to Gallant. *He must have seen it*. Gallant **winced**, shifted on his feet and looked away. *He must have seen the darkness on my heart*. Sir Francis hadn't said anything about it yet, but now Gallant began to wonder if the knight might read his heart during dinner, right in front of the whole family.

William stood next to his wife, smiling tenderly at her. "You remember Catherine," he said to Sir Francis, "she could outrun all of us to the village well." Catherine **curtsied** as she held out one edge of her skirt. It was a polite greeting for a friend she had not seen in many years. When last they shared a meal, he was a mere youth with an eager laugh and a willingness to help anyone in need.

Sir Francis bowed to her and smiled. "Indeed, I do. If only there had been a prize for the fastest runner of the town. God save you, Lady Catherine. It is my pleasure to share your company again." Sir Francis noticed Catherine's eyes, still the glistening blue of a clear sky, with facets of sparkle whenever she smiled. Her hair was lighter than he remembered, likely the result of her work outside in the sun; and she had not aged at all in their years apart.

Catherine blushed. "God save you, Sir Francis. I always knew you two let me win those races. It meant I got to drink from the well first. Even back then, you were gentlemen." She excused herself then, "I really must tend to the pottage, it wouldn't do to serve ill-prepared food to such a special guest." She returned to the boiling kettle, Timothy trailing behind, still clutching a handful of her skirt.

"Ah!" Sir Francis announced suddenly. "Excuse me a moment, lest I forget later." He stepped outside and headed for his horse, which he had left near the wood pile. Gallant watched him through the open doorway. The knight removed his horse's pack and its saddle and blanket and set it on the ground, leaving the animal free to graze near the home. He pulled a worn, patched blanket from the pack and tucked it under his arm. Then he untied leather strips and pulled out the sword William had used earlier. He wiped it clean with the edge of his tunic as he returned to the house. Crossing the threshold, he caught sight of Margaret, whose wide eyes were focused on the sword, even as her little fist clenched the ginger candy.

Gallant knew what her expression meant. *Uh-oh. She's scared.* He tried to distract her. "How is your ginger-sweet, Margie? Do you like it? Don't eat too much before supper!" His plan worked. Margaret turned her attention back to her candy and popped the whole piece into her mouth, chewing as she grinned a toothy, drooling smile.

Sir Francis addressed Gallant: "Kindly place your father's sword out of the way." Both Gallant and William looked quickly at Sir Francis. Margaret clutched her father's neck tightly and closed her eyes with all her might. She even stopped chewing. Catherine paused at the stew pot to listen, then set the butter and the bowls on the table, trying to temper her curiosity.

"My sword?" William asked with great surprise.

Sir Francis responded calmly, "I mean to leave it here. I expect you'll have need of it someday."

William looked puzzled by the comment, but Sir Francis did not elaborate. Instead, he turned to Gallant and offered him the handle of the sword. Gallant looked quickly to his father for permission. When William nodded, he eagerly grasped the sword with two hands. Margaret peeked with one eye. The moment Sir Francis let go, the sword dipped to the ground. It was far heavier than it looked. Gallant pursed his lips as he struggled to steady it. With a grunt, he carried it to a corner and propped it against the wall.

The immediate danger now past, Margaret was back to chewing her candy with vigor and eagerly watching all the commotion. Her view was so much better up high, as she sat perched on her father's forearm one moment; hanging **precariously** over his shoulder the next.

"My friend, I bid you: Be as comfortable in our home, as you would in your own," William said to the knight, bowing slightly and waving his hand across the room.

Sir Francis stepped inside and closed the door, leaning down to place his blanket on the ground out of the way. He **surveyed** the one room house. The floors were dirt, leveled and packed firm, covered by several plain woven rugs in the walkways and under the furniture. A wooden **trestle** table occupied the center of the room, a bench on each long side and a stool at either end. Its light golden hue suggested it had been recently assembled from newly hewn oak boards, and then carefully rubbed with beeswax to seal the wood and protect the top surface against spills. Green-glazed pottery dotted the shelves of a cupboard, and an aged wooden chest with hammered black iron hardware sat neatly in a corner, next to a large box-shaped wooden loom.

Along one wall, three cotton mattresses, stuffed with a rough wool called flock, rested on separate wood frames that had been strung with ropes. The bed in the corner was set apart from the others by a tall, movable "L" shaped wooden frame, similar to a wall partition, over which a linen sheet had been draped. This gave privacy to Catherine and William when they changed their clothes or discussed information not meant for the children to hear.

Sir Francis drew near to the loom to observe Catherine's work. A nearly-finished **tapestry** was stretched taut between the roller arms. Her design involved an intricate pattern of flowering vines woven around a wooden door with no handle. The knight immediately recognized the image as a secret door that allowed a king's friends into a castle under siege. Hidden behind the greenery, the heavy timber door was only accessible to those who knew where to look and how to signal a request for entry.

Sir Francis examined the deep forest green thread loaded into the **weaver's shuttle** and observed that Catherine had used the rich, dark color to form the shaded leaves. "Exquisite!" Sir Francis exclaimed.

Catherine smiled. "You are most kind," she said simply.

Like most women, Catherine could sew, using linen or cotton fabric she obtained in town by trading produce, milk, cheese or eggs. The family also benefited from two dozen sheep, whose wool they sheared twice a year; and it was Catherine's woolen work that was so highly prized by the locals. Looms were rare and not often available to farmers; and those who had them catered to wealthy villagers. Only a few could afford the costly material and dyes necessary for such artistic pieces. Catherine had a skill at the loom that meant she was never without a project.

Next to the loom, a basket overflowed with hand-wound balls of thread spun from the wool of the sheep. The vast variety of colors in the basket reflected the dyes Catherine had created from local leaves, roots, spices, and nut shells. The purple and crimson were imported from far eastern lands, acquired by a clergyman for a tapestry meant to hang in Bristol's magnificent church.

"My eyes bring me to the loom, but my stomach takes me to the pottage!" The knight walked to the other end of the room where steam rose from a black kettle. A metal frame kept the cauldron suspended over a cluster of logs, half burnt and rimmed with white ash. Near the fire, a loaf of bread was set on a grate, being heated for their meal. Sir Francis reached for the ladle and stirred the pot, leaning closer to smell the cooking stew.

"Mmmm. The castle may have expensive and exotic foods, but there is nothing quite as satisfying as pottage on the farm!" The knight bowed to Catherine.

Light streamed into the house through the glass windows, illuminating the center table, now set for a meal. With supper ready to be served,

Catherine moved to a small table near the door, holding a linen towel just above a pewter water basin. Her courteous action alerted Sir Francis that he was being invited to wash his hands and face before they ate.

"Your hospitality is worthy of a king!" He hurried over and washed, graciously accepting the towel from Catherine after a quick splash in the water. Gallant and William washed up next and then all met at the table for supper. William wrapped his hand in a thick cloth and carried the pottage to the table, setting the kettle near Catherine. He turned back to the cooking pit and plucked the dark rye loaf from the grate with a long iron fork, dropping it on a hammered pewter plate in the center of the table.

With all the food now set out, William took his place on a stool, with Catherine on a bench to his right and Sir Francis on the stool at the far end of the table. The children sat on the benches, Timothy next to his mother, and Gallant and Margaret side by side on the opposite bench.

William closed his eyes and prayed words of gratitude: "Lord of all created things, we give you thanks for our faith, our family, our friends and our food. In all things, may we serve you and give you glory, until we attain to our heavenly abode."

Everyone responded: "Amen," and then Catherine filled the wooden bowls with bread William tore from the loaf. The children sat motionless, as they had been taught, waiting for their portion to be handed to them. Gallant watched the vegetables splash out over the black iron ladle onto the bread in each bowl: cabbage, onions, garbanzo beans, peas and even small bits of dry bread from a previous meal. Gallant wasn't fond of beans; but only once had he complained. His father swiftly sent him to bed with no dinner.

"When you appreciate the effort your mother expended in bringing these vegetables to table, you will eat again," his father had said. It was the last time Gallant ever complained about a meal.

Catherine finished distributing the vegetables and broth. The meat came to the bowls last, ensuring everyone a fair portion; but also highlighting the best part of the meal. Steam rose in short curls from each serving as Gallant passed the bowls around the table. When they were all in place, he leaned over and stirred the broth in the bowl in front of Margaret, allowing the air movement to cool the meat and broth and save her delicate mouth.

Timothy placed his ginger next to his bowl and waited patiently while Catherine cooled his serving. Gallant noticed Margaret eying his piece of candy, rocking just out of her arm's reach. *I'll bet she wished she had waited to eat hers!* She always enjoyed her sweet as soon as she received it, while Timothy delighted in saving his for later, happy to carry a treat around in his pocket for hours or even days.

William tore another swatch of the loaf for everyone. The stew now sufficiently cooled, Timothy and Margaret dipped their bread into their bowls and began to eat it, soaked and squishy. Gallant spooned out a section of butter, placing it in the middle of his chunk of bread and watching it melt down into the steaming center.

Catherine poured cups of spiced honey water for the children and mugs of ale for the adults, and then she sat down at the table to join them, just as William urged Sir Francis to share his stories. Everyone waited eagerly for him to begin, trying to minimize the clanging of their spoons and cups, so as not to disturb the storyteller.

"Alas! The era when knights would battle in full armor has all but vanished," Sir Francis began. "Once weapons could pierce the metal at long distances, the heavy and expensive suits gave way to lighter garments and more sophisticated warfare. Still, we train young men in the ways of the knight in order to impart discipline and honor; and we continue the combat and the pageantry of the tournament to test their progress and entertain the king—and the crowds."

Sir Francis took several bites of his pottage. "Delicious!" He set his spoon down and reached for the piece of bread next to his bowl, lathering a slab of butter across the top of it. "Many valiant men have passed before us, knights of old whose tales we tell, even now, so many years later. We benefit from their worthy lives only when we pass on the memory of their heroic actions. The good we carry forward to imitate. The bad we strive to avoid. Ah. There is much I could say. What would you hear?"

William held up his hand. "Indulge us with news of the tournaments. Do they still draw the best fighters from outside England?"

Sir Francis continued. "Indeed. They come from the territory of Burgundy and from Saxony,

France, Spain and Scotland to challenge the best of our English fighters. The competitions are certainly games of strength and skill between the knights." He glanced at Catherine. "And more than one has settled the dispute among men for the hand of a fair lady! But they have also become **exhibitions** of the most elaborate engravings of metal as well as the newest techniques in **forging.**"

Gallant hung on every word, but Timothy was more interested in his meal. He began to slurp, tipping the bowl at the edge of the table to catch the small puddle at the bottom. Catherine set the bowl aright and poured another ladle of broth to quiet him.

As Sir Francis detailed the recent championship **joust**, Gallant and William bent forward in their seats to hear every word, while Catherine leaned back and turned her head; as if, in doing so, she might avoid the danger.

In the story, when Sir Francis and the knight on horseback clashed, Sir Francis suddenly clapped his hands together to emphasize the smashing of his jousting pole on the other knight's shoulder. "It was as though the holy angels guided me," Sir Francis continued, "a perfect strike; and down

he came, his horse running on without a rider!"
Sir Francis was naturally inclined to smile and he
often added a wink for emphasis when he spoke to
the children.

"Well done!" William exclaimed as he lifted
his **tankard** in salute. "What was the prize?"

"A **sounder of swine**, and enough acorns to
feed them until late summer harvest," Sir Francis
responded proudly. "Of course, the banquet was
nearly a prize in itself. The wine flowed so freely
that the Bishop ordered the barrels to be capped
at the seventh course of the meal. No doubt he
prevented more than a few drunken brawls."

Everyone delighted in Sir Francis' storytell-
ing; a descriptive mix of colorful adventure and
little-known history which entertained both children and adults. At dusk, William lowered the
wooden shutters over the windows, as Catherine
lit a tall slender yellow beeswax candle and placed
it in the center of the table. They rejoined the
knight, eager for more stories.

Gallant watched the light dance over the
faces. The flame flickered with each wave of Sir
Francis' hand and twice it nearly went out when
he leaned close to the candle and whispered the
critical ending of a mock battle.

After the first few tales, William and Catherine took turns contributing to the discussion; giving Sir Francis the opportunity to eat while his food was still hot. By the time they had discussed the sheep, the tapestries, the produce, the townsfolk, and then asked about the king and his noblemen, the conversation had continued long past dessert. With the sweet sauce of the bread pudding still in their mouths, Timothy and Margaret crawled off to their bed; while Gallant remained at the table with the adults, daydreaming he had gone to the festival with Sir Francis.

Gallant closed his eyes and saw the bright gold and bold blues of the banners waving in the summer breeze, just as Sir Francis described them. He imagined an armor-clad knight on an enormous snorting black horse had asked him to hold a sword while the knight took his turn at the joust. It was getting late in the evening and Gallant had nodded off, his head propped on his hand, his elbow on the edge of the table.

"You are excused, Gallant," Catherine said. Hearing his name jolted him awake. "You may say your evening prayers in bed." He stood, thanked his mother and father for the meal, and thanked Sir Francis for his stories. Then he bowed as he had been taught and turned to his mattress. He was grateful for the wonderful stories but even more relieved Sir Francis did not read his heart out loud during dinner. *Maybe he will tell them after I've gone to bed, but there's nothing to be done about it now.*

Gallant was too tired to worry. He took off his shoes, outer shirt and pants and climbed under the covers. Six months ago, William and Gallant assembled the third wooden frame so Gallant would have his own cot. He eagerly stuffed the cotton mattress cover with flock while Catherine sewed together several layers of cotton and linen to create a warm blanket. Now that he wasn't sharing a bed with his younger siblings, he didn't wake them when he went to sleep later or when he rose early to help with the chores.

"It has been a delight to visit with you, Sir Francis." The moment Catherine moved to stand, Sir Francis also stood, bowing to her.

"Thank you for a most delicious meal," he said. Catherine wished her best to Sir Francis and kissed William, who was also now standing. "God save you," Sir Francis called out as she stepped behind the wall partition to prepare for bed.

William and Sir Francis sat down at the table and continued to talk long into the night. Gallant could hear the two men **murmuring** and he could see the candle light playing on the wall. His eyes slowly dropped shut and he began to doze.

"I've always wanted to repay you for your kindness, William," Gallant heard Sir Francis tell his father. Gallant turned on his side, the ropes of his bed creaking under the movement. *I wonder what Father did to make Sir Francis so grateful.* He pulled the blanket over his ear, too sleepy to listen.

The steady voice of his father came in response: "One does not engage in kindness in order to be repaid. One does what is right, and if it happens to be looked upon as kind, well, so be it."

"Saving a life is no small kindness," Sir Francis responded. "Now that Gallant is a young man and I am free of my former obligations, I have returned to share my knowledge of knighthood with him. It is the type of training he would not otherwise receive."

Gallant's eyes popped open. *What? A knight wants to train me, a farmer's boy, to be a knight? But that never happens. Only the children of knights are trained as knights.* Gallant thought he was dreaming.

Sir Francis continued, "He's a sharp boy, quick on his feet, eager and brave. He's well formed, even advanced for his age. I tell you, William, he is a worthy candidate."

For a moment, William was silent, then he spoke slowly. Gallant thought he could hear a note of sadness in his voice. "Gallant assists me in the fields and helps me care for the animals. I could not manage without him."

Sir Francis **countered** quickly: "Just a half day of lessons twice a week, then. He'd be done by noon."

William replied, "There is the matter of your payment."

"Yes, but—" Sir Francis tried to speak but his words trailed off. Gallant supposed his father had held up his hand to silence him.

William spoke firmly. "The offer will not otherwise be considered."

Sir Francis was quiet for a moment before he replied. "Everyone knows you have the warmest wool in the territory and Catherine's work surpasses any other weaver. A blanket, then, with wool from your sheep, spun and woven by your wife. That will be ample payment."

Gallant closed his eyes. *It's impossible, really. Farm boys do not become knights.* During another pause in the conversation, he pulled the covers closer around him. Just as he started to doze off, he heard his father call out in a raised voice, "So this is why you have left us with a sword. Very well, then. One day there will be a young knight in this household, and we shall call him Sir Gallant!"

1. Why did Sir Francis ask Gallant to describe how they built their house if Sir Francis already knew the answer?

2. What if someone could read your heart? Would that bother you?

fathom (sounds like **fath**-um): a noun, equal to six feet, a term later used almost exclusively for nautical (sea) measurements

horizontal (sounds like hore-i-**zon**-tall): an adjective, to be parallel to the ground

reeds (sounds like **reeds**): a noun, a plant that grows in marshy areas; their tough stalks were woven together and used for many purposes, including paper, mats, and roofs

winced (sounds like **winssd**): a verb, to squint the eyes and pull away, as from something scary or painful

curtsied (sounds like **kurt**-seed): a verb, a type of bow given by girls and women to show respect and appreciation

precariously (sounds like pree-**carry**-us-lee): an adverb, dangerously, with risk

surveyed (sounds like sur-**vaid**): a verb, to look around carefully, to take note of surroundings

trestle (sounds like **tress**-l): an adjective, a type of framework that supports a long table

tapestry (sounds like **tap**-uh-stree): a noun, a sturdy woven cloth containing images or designs in colored thread, used for wall-hangings or covering furniture

weaver (sounds like **weve**-r): a noun, a person who creates cloth by crisscrossing threads on a loom

shuttle (sounds like **shuh**-tull): a noun, a small device to hold thread as it moves back and forth across a loom

exhibition (sounds like ex-ih-**bih**-shon): a noun, a display or show

forging (sounds like **forj**-ing): a noun, the process of creating metal using high heat and a hammer

joust (sounds like **jow**-st): a noun, a contest where two knights on horseback use long poles to try to knock the other off his horse

tankard (sounds like **tank**-ard): a noun, a sturdy mug made of metal

sounder of swine (sounds like **sound**-her): a noun, a group of pigs

murmuring (sounds like **murr**-murr-ing): noun, quiet talking

countered (sounds like **koun**-terd): a verb, to propose an idea different than the one discussed

If you have the Sir Gallant Castle Kit, go to your Workbook now and complete the next lesson, called Banner 2.

CHAPTER THREE

Another Chance to be Good

The next morning when Gallant awoke, Sir Francis was gone and Gallant's family had returned to their routine. It was Sunday, so they only did the necessary work. From the stalls behind the house, the sheep and goats bleated their irritation as William milked them; and within a few minutes, Catherine returned to the house with several logs pinched together in a wide leather strap she held at both ends. The strap normally hung on a peg by the door, readily accessible to the family for their many trips outside to the wood pile.

Catherine knelt at the fire pit and scraped the ash aside with a small flat black iron shovel. Blowing on the glowing embers underneath, she added the wood pieces one at a time, careful not to smother the newly emerging flame. As she hung a pot of water over the fire, the fresh timber began to snap. The combination of sounds woke the children. Margaret and Timothy sat up, yawning and waiting for Catherine to notice and call a morning greeting.

William had opened the window shutters before he left to milk the goats, and now the morning sun was peeking through the window, forming a shaft of light that streamed into the room. Gallant sat up in his bed and scratched his head, wondering if Sir Francis really meant to teach him the ways of a knight. He stared at the specks of dust dancing in the beam of light. *Maybe it was all just a dream.* He reached for the edge of his blanket and fell back onto his pillow, just as his father entered the house and placed the wooden buckets of milk onto the trestle table. "Up, Gallant," his father called loudly. "This is the day which the Lord hath made!" With a grin, he added: "A knight does not waste away his days in bed."

Gallant sprang off his bed, suddenly wide awake. He ran to William. "What are you saying, Father?"

William sat on a bench and motioned his son nearer. "Sir Francis has offered to instruct you in exchange for one of your mother's finest wool blankets," he told the boy. "He will stay at Bristol's inn for the summer. Twice each week, he will visit our farm and meet you in the storehouse for a half-day lesson."

"Oh! What else? What do I—" Gallant was stopped in mid-sentence. He could see his father was not interested in explaining all the details just then.

"Enough," William announced. "We must turn our hearts to God now." Like most villagers, Gallant's parents were very serious about their obligation to God.

"Good morning, my ginger-sweets!" Catherine sat on the bed with the two little ones and gently pushed Margaret's hair out of her eyes. She pulled back the children's covers and helped them to the table, beginning a Sunday routine to which they all had grown accustomed. After a breakfast of warm milk and boiled eggs, Catherine scrubbed the children's faces and ears, and they were each given a **sprig** of mint to chew on. She helped to dress the little ones, while Gallant tossed out the water from the wash basin and brought a bucket of fresh water from the well, refilling the basin and leaving the bucket with the remaining water near the fire for his mother's cooking. William prepared the horse-drawn wagon to take them all to Bristol's cathedral.

On the way into town, everyone kept a respectful silence, just as they had been taught. Well, mostly. Margaret and Timothy made each other giggle, and Catherine would hold her finger to her mouth to shush them. "Consider God's great blessings and prepare a place in your hearts to welcome your Savior." But today as they bounced along in the wagon on the way to church, Gallant was having a hard time concentrating on anything except the knight lessons.

When he closed his eyes, he could picture knights in his mind because he had seen them at the fairs. But he could not picture God. *How do I welcome someone I have never met?* He thought this understanding would come as he grew older, but now he didn't have time to wait. Gallant knew that training to be a knight had changed everything.

"What does that mean, Mother? How do we welcome our Savior?" Gallant asked earnestly.

His mother turned to Gallant as he rode in the rear of the wagon. "Imagine Jesus were coming to our home for supper. In your mind, set the table, draw fresh water for the wash basin, set a bowl at the head of the table. Prepare for the King of kings to arrive. Watch for Him and when he enters, sit at His feet and talk to Him." His mother hugged Timothy, who sat on her knee. "Thank the Lord for His many gifts. Praise Him. Ask Him for the things you need and tell Him you will try to make up for your past errors."

"And then listen for His response?" Gallant was beginning to understand. They had just welcomed Sir Francis for dinner the night before and it was still fresh in his mind.

"Yes, dear one. Prayer is just a conversation with holy God. Now that you are training to be a knight, you will have much to talk about with 'Dominus Deus Sabaoth'—the Lord God of the Armies!" Gallant's mouth dropped open. *I never thought of Him that way!*

When they arrived at the church courtyard, William tied the reins of their horse to a post and helped Catherine and Timothy down, while

Gallant gazed at the building from its **foundation** all the way to its pointed **spires**. The church was an enormous, magnificent Gothic structure constructed with blocks of tan stone. Gallant heard that before lightning had struck the spire seventy years ago, sailors could see the peak of the church from miles away on the river Avon.

The bolt of lightning started a fire that caused the soaring spire to collapse, bringing down two-thirds of it and causing damage to the church interior. What was left reminded Gallant of a carrot broken off in the middle. The town often spoke of rebuilding it, but several nobles contended about the repair. Since it would require a significant sum of money, the potential benefactors wished to have assurances that the new structure would not be damaged in the same way in the future.

Gallant hopped down from the back of the wagon and reached for Margaret, carefully setting her on the ground and taking her hand. As they walked, he thought about the broken spire. *Perhaps Sir Henry will devise a solution.* Proceeding up the entrance stairs, Gallant recalled that glorious day last October at the Festival of St. Crispin. Master Henry Somerset was knighted at this very church, St. Mary Redcliffe. William and Gallant had attended the ceremony, an event that drew nearly all the local townsfolk.

When Sir Henry emerged from the church on that brisk fall day, he stood at the top of the wide stone staircase, his helmet under one arm and a pole in the other. The red and white coat-of-arms he had chosen was emblazoned on his **tabard** and on the **standard** tied to the top of his pole. His armor glinted in the sun and a soft breeze lifted the fabric of his flag so that it flapped gently. *What a sight!* Gallant imagined Sir Henry standing on the battlefield over his defeated enemy. The crowd outside the church greeted him, waving their hats and cheering, "Sir Henry! Sir Henry!"

Sir Henry waited a few moments and then raised his pole, signaling his intention to speak. The crowd quieted. "By God's grace was I knighted," he said solemnly. "A year with the monks prepared me for this honor, but last night, during my vigil of prayer on my knees before the altar, the Lord confirmed He had given me the heart of a knight. May it be that I serve Him well." Gallant tried to recall the oath Sir Henry had taken. *Something about loyalty and courage and humility*, he remembered, *a devotion to Jesus Christ and to the perfect ideals he taught.*

Gallant's family joined the others as they all filed past the thick wooden doors into the grand church and found a place in the central open area. After being in the morning sunlight, Gallant needed a few moments for his eyes to adjust to the indoors. He paused to admire the symmetry of multiple archways down the length and across the width of the church. More than eight fathoms above him, the ceiling was decorated with ornate wood moldings that joined in beautiful patterns, arriving in points where the archways met with the fluted pillars.

The church was usually warm in the summer and very cold in the winter. Light pierced through the windows, illuminating colorful stained glass scenes from the Bible. Those depicting prophets, such as Noah and Moses, were drawn from the Old Testament; whereas the images of the life of Jesus and his mother, Mary, were taken from the New Testament. Once a month, the priest used these images to instruct the people about the faith.

Candles burned at the altar, but only a few pillar **sconces** lit the area where the people gathered. Since no benches or chairs were available for the congregants, the people stood or kneeled on the stone floor for the entire service. Sometimes

Gallant's little brother and sister would be allowed to lie down on their mother's cape, but Gallant was old enough that he was expected to stay awake and pray. His mother often reminded the family they had much for which they should be grateful: healthy sheep and goats, good crops, a warm and safe home, and each other.

Bristol was the third-largest city in England, and it was very **prosperous**. A section at the front of the church had been reserved for the **benefactors**, and several leading men of the town, including the Mayor of Bristol, had earned the honor through their large contributions. As the people filed past Gallant, he noticed the difference in their attire. The wealthy, who were either nobility or successful businessmen, wore clothes made of colorful and expensive fabrics. The rich ladies in church wore long dresses and shimmering veils; the men wore fancy jackets and tall boots. This group stood near the front, closest to the altar. But even they did not dare to pass the railing and enter the space reserved for the priest—an area called the **sanctuary**.

On this particular Sunday, Gallant was able to see along the edge of the people ahead of him, because an area like a hallway down the center of the church remained open. This was done on purpose, a symbolic act of people who awaited the return of Jesus.

A chime rang out, signaling the beginning of the Mass. Gallant peered all the way down the center aisle and carefully watched the priest and his two assistants as they knelt a moment facing the altar and the **tabernacle**, their backs to the people. The men were dressed in vestments, exquisitely embroidered religious robes made of silk.

As the priest stood, a collection of voices joined together from the rear of the church to sing. The schola-master led the choir in the chanting, a specific type of singing reserved for religious events. The singing wasn't the kind Gallant's mother did, it was more like talking but in a calm and steady rhythm. The voices were rich and deep and the chant echoed through the church. The choir paused while the priest and his assistants continued with the prayers of the Mass, which were sometimes silent and sometimes audible to the people.

The priest and his assistants moved in a deliberate way, lining up one behind the other on the stairs of the altar and taking off their black, tufted caps at the same time whenever "Iesu Christi"

(Latin for Jesus Christ) was spoken or sung. The people watched for this gesture and they bowed or bent their knee as soon as they saw it. The priests at St. Mary Redcliffe often reminded the people: "Scripture tells us 'That in the name of Jesus every knee should bow, of those that are in heaven, on earth, and under the earth.'" The action was not frivolous, it was required. Gallant was learning how each movement of the priest conveyed a lesson about the faith.

A distinctive scent drifted through the church. The priest was waving a metal lantern called a thurible, which hung from several chains, as smoke came out and drifted upward. Gallant knew this was **incense**. Last Sunday on the wagon ride home, Father had explained to the children that as the incense rose to the ceiling, it reminded the congregation that the angels were carrying their prayers to God in Heaven.

Gallant added his knight prayer to the incense; but then he noticed the shoemaker and his wife across the aisle. Gallant's mother had mentioned them during the family's evening prayer a couple days earlier. Their newborn son died shortly after birth, and they mourned the loss. Gallant asked God to comfort them—and not just them, but every parent who had lost a child. He remembered the many times his mother had reminded him, "God loves when we pray for each other, especially when we remember those who are hurting."

Timothy started to giggle. He had seen a twig on his father's pant leg and every time he tried to reach for it, his father moved just enough so that Timothy would miss. It got to be a game, and now Margaret was watching. Gallant could see she was about to burst into laughter. Just then, the choir began to sing again. Timothy and Margaret stopped fidgeting and stretched to see the singers. Gallant closed his eyes and wondered if this was what the holy angels sounded like. The choir sang in Latin, the ancient language of the church:

> *Familiam tuam, quaesumus, Domine,*
> *continua pietate custodi:*
> *ut a cunctis adversitatibus,*
> *te protegente, sit libera:*
> *et in bonis actibus tuo nomini sit devota.*
> *Per Dominum nostrum.*

Gallant thought back to a conversation he had overheard just outside the church. Two of the wealthy patrons were conferring with one another, and a small group of the faithful had gathered around them to listen.

"Why Latin?" A younger man in a green velvet cape inquired of an older man.

"Latin is no longer used in conversation," the older fellow responded. A large medallion hanging around his neck indicated he was highly educated, likely a tutor to the children of the nobles. He continued, raising a finger for emphasis. "Thus, the meaning of the words will never vary. When brought over to the common tongue, the prayer retains its original meaning."

The younger man had nodded thoughtfully. "Ah, yes! Using a language that does not change to teach about an unchanging God."

Well, that makes sense, Gallant thought at the time. He had heard that the town of Bristol had originally been called Brygestowe, and later was known as Bristowe. It was modified because the language of the people developed over the years. *If the name had originally been Latin, it would have been the same 500 years ago and 500 years from now.*

All respectable villagers attended Mass every Sunday. During the service, they followed the movement of the priests and the ringing of the bells as clues to what was being said. When the priest once again incensed the altar, it was a sign to the people that a passage would be read from one of the four Gospels, the stories of the life of Jesus. After the Gospel was read, the priest climbed the stairs of the dark wood pulpit, an impressive structure ringed about with exquisitely carved statues of holy saints. Elevated above the people, he was easily seen and heard as he issued words of counsel based on the Gospel reading. The sermon, as it was called, was always in the native language of the people.

"THOU SHALT NOT STEAL!" The priest began with a loud and forceful command, startling Gallant because the priest seemed to be looking straight at him with piercing black eyes. Gallant stared at his feet and then slowly took a step behind his mother, so he was partially hidden from the priest by her long skirt. His face suddenly grew very hot. *How did the priest know what I did?*

"Do you STEAL if you allow your scales to remain unbalanced?" the priest called out sharply. "Do you STEAL if you quote different prices to the rich and the poor?" He paused dramatically as he slowly passed his gaze over the entire gathering. "Yes! I say, yes indeed! There is no room for duplicity if you wish to follow the

Savior. 'Love thy neighbor!' Jesus commanded. 'Be kind to those who persecute you.' We do not STEAL from those we LOVE, do we? Nor should you STEAL from your persecutors! Woe to you who disregard the words of the Christ! Will you be spared? NO! You will be thrust down to the very fires of Gehenna, where the worm dies not and the flame is never extinguished!"

Gallant noticed the man in front of him was twisting his hat in his hands and shuffling from foot to foot. Gallant got distracted watching a little boy who was crawling around one of the **pillars**, chasing some kind of bug. Before he knew it, the priest had stopped talking and the service was moving on.

At Communion time, only a few brave souls dared to venture forward to receive the Host—a small, thin circle of bread over which special prayers had been said. It was the size of a coin, and the priest placed it on the tongue of those who knelt at the railing. Gallant was told this Host was Jesus Himself, God, the King of Heaven and Earth, but he didn't quite understand how such a thing was possible. *Still, Jesus being God and all, He could do whatever He wanted.* In that sense, it was quite simple.

Like most of the people of the time, Gallant's parents only received Communion once a year at Christmas time, although sometimes they made an exception for special feast days like St. Swithin's. The church taught that receiving the Host unworthily was such a serious sin that a person could lose his or her soul if they died without repenting. The people took the warning seriously, often fasting and praying for months before receiving Communion.

Gallant thought of that summer afternoon, not long ago, when he and his father were out collecting firewood. "Why take the Host at all," the boy had asked, "if you risk being sent to the eternal fire?"

His father was quick with the answer. "Scripture tells us: 'Except you eat the flesh of the Son of man, and drink his blood, you shall not have life in you.'" William had stopped chopping wood, just to emphasize the seriousness of his response. "It is because of His love for us that Jesus requires it, son. And so we work hard to be worthy. It is the nearest to God we can be, this side of Heaven."

The last of the faithful who had received the Host left the railing and returned to their places. Following Communion, the priest offered more prayers and read from the beginning of the Gospel of John, which signaled the end of Mass. Gallant watched as the priest and his assistants processed out of the sanctuary and into the **sacristy**. Slowly and quietly, the people began to file out of the church. Out of respect for the Lord in the tabernacle, no one turned his back to the altar. Those in the front stepped sideways to an exit. Those near the rear of the church backed out. Gallant took Margaret's hand and followed his family, mulling over what the priest had said.

Gallant had prayed to be a good knight, and the priest gave a fearful message about stealing. *It was God's way of speaking to me. I was wrong to take something that did not belong to me.* Gallant wasn't sure how to fix what he had done, but he planned to pray and ask God to help him. He remembered the priest had said in a previous sermon that God speaks in whispers, so he planned to stay as quiet as he could to try to hear what God would say to him.

Although Gallant was distracted, he found the ride home from church pleasant. Catherine was humming part of a chant, and William occasionally looked over and blew her a kiss. When they got home, William was ready to tell Gallant more about the teaching arrangement they had made with Sir Francis.

Think About This

1. Why does going to church help many people to be good?

2. Gallant made a mistake he knew he needed to fix. Have you made any mistakes you would like to fix?

Word Helper

sprig (sounds like **sprig**): a noun, a small branch, a piece of a plant

foundation (sounds like fown-**day**-shun): a noun, the base on which something is built

spires (sounds like **spy**-rs): a noun, tall narrow points at the top of buildings

tabard (sounds like **tab**-erd): a noun, a decorative shirt worn over chain mail or armor bearing a knight's colors and coat-of-arms

standard (sounds like **stan**-dard): a noun, a flag bearing significant colors or figures

sconces (sounds like **skaun**-says): a noun, wall-mounted lights or candle-holders

prosperous (sounds like **pros**-purr-us): an adjective, wealthy, successful in business

benefactor (sounds like **ben**-nah-**fack**-tore): a noun, someone who donates money or helps others

sanctuary (sounds like **sank**-tew-airy): a noun, the area in a church closest to the altar, where the priest stands to celebrate Mass

tabernacle (sounds like **tab**-er-**nack**-ull): a noun, a fancy box or container used to hold Hosts

incense (sounds like **inn**-cents): a noun, a powder burned for its fragrance

pillar (sounds like **pill**-lar): a noun, a post that holds up the roof

sacristy (sounds like **sack**-chris-tee): a noun, the room used by a priest to prepare for Mass

---

If you have the Sir Gallant Castle Kit, go to your Workbook now and complete the next lesson, called Banner 3.

CHAPTER FOUR

A Dragon Goes to School

Much **preparation** was necessary before the knight training could begin. Gallant helped his mother clear excess timber from an area in the storeroom so both he and Sir Francis had a place to sit during class. William used the wood to build some rough furniture for the makeshift classroom: two tables, a bench, a chair, and a **lectern**. Sir Francis would return in one month's time, and Gallant was to be awake, washed, dressed, and waiting with his slate board and chalk in the storeroom by break of day. Gallant was thrilled.

It wasn't too difficult to convince Timothy to find small stones they could use to count the days before Sir Francis would return. (Timothy loved to collect stones.) When they had thirty, Gallant put them in a pile by his bed. Every morning when he awoke, he took one stone and threw it outside. Timothy learned the routine soon after it started, so he waited until Gallant tossed the stone, and then he went and retrieved it to place it in his own stone collection. Gallant still had to tend the sheep and complete his chores in addition to all this new activity.

And now that he would be training for knighthood, he knew he had to bring prayer into his daily routine. He decided to join his prayer to the chores he did when he was alone. *That way, I won't forget to say them.* As he stacked the firewood next to the house, each piece represented a different person. "Lord, please bless my father with health and strength. Bless my mother with joy and peace. Bless Margaret and Timothy and keep them safe."

As he swept out the barn with their scraggly straw broom, he asked God to help him sweep out every bad behavior from his heart. He soon found that the more carefully he said his prayers, the more thoroughly he completed his chores.

Even with all his best efforts dedicated to the preparations, the month still dragged. Finally only one stone was left by Gallant's bed. That night, he could barely sleep. When he finally dozed off, he dreamed about wearing armor and riding on an enormous white horse. In his dream, he slayed a dragon threatening the poor villagers and the grateful townspeople held a hero's parade to thank him.

"Sir Gallant! Sir Gallant!" they cheered as the women threw flowers at his feet.

"Gallant!" It wasn't the villagers calling anymore, it was his mother. "Did you mean to sleep this late?"

The morning sun had already tipped its way into the house when Gallant opened his eyes. If it had reached into the window, Gallant knew it was past the break of day. "Oh no!" he cried out. "Late, on my first day of school!" He threw back his blanket and dressed for school, with scarcely enough time to splash his face and drag a rough comb across his hair. He couldn't find his shoes, and when he tucked his slate board under his arm, it still bore the drawing of a dragon he had created to **entertain** his brother the night before. *A fine knight I shall be when I can't even dress myself in time.* Gallant ran from corner to corner in the farm house before he finally found his shoes next to the fire pit, right where he had left them the night before. He pulled one shoe on and hopped toward the door as he pulled on the other one.

"Goodbye, mother!" He dashed out the door and across the field, startling a wild turkey that had wandered in his path. Gallant recognized Sir Francis' horse grazing near the storehouse. As he neared the building where his classes were to be taught, he heard a voice speaking forcefully from within. *How odd. Sir Francis has been hired as my tutor, and I am his only student.* Gallant slowed to a walk and wiped a bead of sweat from his forehead as he pulled open the large wooden door.

Just then, Sir Francis raised his voice and pointed his finger straight up to the ceiling for emphasis. "And THAT is the quickest and surest way to become a knight!" Gallant looked around the room slowly. Sir Francis was speaking to an empty room! Gallant blinked his eyes **deliberately** and looked again. No, he was sure. There was no one except Sir Francis in the room. But Sir Francis had just given the greatest lesson of all!

"What is it, Sir Francis?" Gallant called out breathlessly as he hurried forward from the back of the room. "What is the surest way to become a knight?" Gallant was on his toes with excitement, it was exactly what he had hoped to learn.

"Sit down, Master Gallant." Sir Francis spoke firmly. "Your class began at daybreak. Therefore you have missed a portion of my lecture. It will not be repeated." Gallant stopped in the middle of the room.

"B-b-but—" he **stammered**, "But I *must* know the surest way to become a knight."

"Sit down." Sir Francis repeated. "And if I must tell you again, you shall acquire your first **demerit**."

Gallant sat down on the floor right where he stood, even though there was a bench and table set up for him in the room. He set his slate board on the ground next to him and then realized his teacher was staring at it. He looked down and felt the heat of embarrassment burning his face. The image of the dragon was still on his board! *Another example of my failure to prepare for school.* Gallant picked up the board and quickly wiped it with the edge of his shirt, smearing the art and leaving his shirt full of white chalk.

Sir Francis began to explain how the class would be taught, and what materials Gallant would need. He talked about the lessons Gallant would learn and the tests he would take.

"When you thoughtfully consider another man's story, you learn as though you walked his path," Sir Francis said, his voice particularly solemn. "You must listen carefully at all times, and you will begin to discern what words should be valued and what words should be discarded. Later in your lessons, you will practice the art of memorizing." Sir Francis looked sternly at his student before he added, "But my goal is to help you to think for yourself and to reason through problems. That is the best preparation for the situations in which a knight will find himself."

Gallant was eager to do knight-things, like sword fighting and jousting, but William had instructed him not to pester Sir Francis about such topics. "Sir Francis will teach you exactly what you need to learn, in the order he deems appropriate," his father had said that Sunday morning, a month ago.

By the time his first class was over, Gallant had made up his mind about a few things. When Sir Francis signaled the end of the class, Gallant stood up and bowed to his teacher, as was customary. Then he picked up his slate board and left the storeroom.

As he walked, he felt ashamed about his failure and angry with himself. He realized he had missed the greatest lesson of all, just because he chose a comfortable bed over the early-morning knight lesson. *It was silly of me to sleep in; and rude to arrive late.* Gallant knew that he had acted as though his own time was more important than Sir Francis' time. Not only that, but in all his rushing, he had forgotten to pray.

The moment he remembered, he stopped in the field and asked the Lord to forgive his failings and assist him in every way to become a true knight. Then he brought out his slate board, wiping away the remains of the dragon with his sleeve. He wrote in bold letters: DON'T BE LATE. "I shall not be late again when someone is expecting me," he said out loud. Then he wrote another line: BE PREPARED. "I will clean my slate board the night before and line up my shoes where I can find them." He began to walk again toward his home.

Just then, the farmhouse door opened and his mother came out to shake the dirt from a rug. She caught sight of Gallant and smiled warmly. Gallant returned the smile, but he was walking slowly, rather ashamed of his behavior. *Just last night, mother encouraged me to get up as soon as I heard father collecting the buckets to milk the sheep and goats.* Gallant always awoke to the sound, but this morning he was warm under his covers, and he was still sleepy, so he had pulled the blanket over his ears to savor just a few more minutes of rest. But because he hadn't slept well all night, he fell back asleep.

The young boy's final promise to himself was his most important. He wrote a third line on his slate board: OBEY MOTHER AND FATHER. "I will never again ignore their instructions," Gallant said, looking at his slate board and nodding with satisfaction. Then he tucked the board under his arm and ran toward his mother, to tell her all about his first day of school. Gallant didn't see Sir Francis standing at the door of the storeroom behind him. But Sir Francis heard Gallant's promises.

"If he can avoid the little mistakes," Sir Francis said to himself, "he can keep clear of the larger ones. The boy is off to a better start than he thinks."

Sir Francis returned to the storeroom, dropped the wood shutter down over the open window, and collected his teaching supplies. As he left the building, he adjusted his satchel on his shoulder and called to his horse. It walked toward him, stopping within his arm's reach. The knight patted the horse's neck firmly. "Soon, my faithful steed, we shall see what this boy is really made of."

Think About This

1. What are the lessons Gallant learned? (Hint: they are in capital letters in the story).

2. Nowadays, some children are sent to a public or private school and some children are schooled in their homes. Whatever your circumstances, what are some things you can do to be ready when class begins?

preparation (sounds like preh-par-**ay**-shun): a noun, the process of making something ready

lectern (sounds like **leck-**turn): a noun, a tall stand used by teachers to hold their papers

entertain (sounds like en-ter-**tayne**): a verb, to amuse

deliberately (sounds like de-**lib**-ur-at-lee): an adverb, to do something very carefully, with much thought

stammered (sounds like **stam**-mer-d): verb, to speak with difficulty

demerit (sounds like dee-**mare**-it): a noun, a mark against someone for committing an error

encouraged (sounds like en-**curr**-aj-d): a verb, to help another person to do something, to cheer them on

If you have the Sir Gallant Castle Kit, go to your Workbook now and complete the next lesson, called Banner 4.

CHAPTER FIVE

The Talking Garden

After several classes, Gallant was beginning to get comfortable with the routine and with his tutor. Sir Francis always began with a prayer before he launched into the day's lesson, and he often included words of wisdom interspersed with his instructions.

On this early-summer morning, Gallant stood in the middle of his mother's cabbage patch and watched the sun rising in the east. He was determined to follow instructions carefully, so when Sir Francis said, "Gallant, we shall meet for our next class at your mother's garden," Gallant knew he needed to be standing in the garden first thing in the morning, instead of sitting at his school desk.

As he waited for Sir Francis, he thought about how blessed he was. *What is it that Mother always sings when she is gardening?* He paused a moment, humming the melody quietly to himself. *Ah yes, I remember.*

> *She considered a field, and bought it:*
> *with the fruit of her hands she planted.*
> *She opened her hand to the needy,*
> *and stretched out her hands to the poor.*

He continued to hum the tune as he looked down the neat rows of cabbages and noticed how carefully his mother had planted them so the rows would be straight. *It certainly makes it easier to clear the weeds.* Just past the cabbage, Gallant noticed the pea plants and saw how their pods were already expanding to hold the peas inside them. They had tender little shoots with curls on each end. Gallant had watched several weeks ago as his mother placed sticks in the ground next to each pea plant. He realized now that the curls had grabbed onto the sticks and caused the plants to climb and grow upward. *How clever! They get more sun stretched out tall, than they would all bunched together and lying on the ground.*

Gallant took a few steps toward the pea plants to get a closer look, but he was distracted by the rows and rows of rye plants. Rye was the grain his mother relied upon to make the hearty, dark bread that was an important part of nearly every meal. After the harvest, Gallant's father would bring his oldest son along to take the grain sacks to the town mill, where the miller would grind it into the fine flour Catherine used to make bread. When the harvest was good, the family had enough flour to last right up until the next season's harvest.

Gallant stepped over the pea plants and across the cabbage, looking curiously at another kind of plant growing in neat rows, spaced about a shoe-length apart. Its red stalks were sprouting large green leaves covered with red veins. He wasn't sure what kind of vegetable this plant would produce, but he recalled seeing the stalks and leaves hanging over the edge of mother's vegetable basket. *Hmmm. Carrots? Onions? Leeks?*

Before he could decide, Sir Francis strolled across the adjacent yard and into the garden. Gallant was looking at the **tilled** soil and just then, an awful memory flooded into his mind. He stopped humming, remembering the day he dug a hole in the dirt near the edge of their property and buried the item he had taken so many months ago. *Sir Francis would be so disappointed if he knew I stole it from a poor widow. I am sorry. I am.* Gallant hadn't heard Sir Francis, and he was lost in his thoughts when the knight arrived just a few steps behind him.

"May the Good Lord bless our efforts and pour His Wisdom upon us as we seek to please Him by our studies. What have you learned so far today, Gallant?" asked Sir Francis.

Gallant was startled by the interruption and bewildered by the question. He spun around to address Sir Francis, trying to put the item out of his mind. *What? What have I learned? Wait, Sir Francis has not taught me anything yet!*

Gallant stared blankly at Sir Francis, who urged him to speak. "Class began on time, just as it always does," Sir Francis said, "and you were walking among the garden plants. Surely you learned something from all your **observations!**"

Gallant looked at the ground and tried to collect his thoughts.

"Well?" Sir Francis seemed eager to begin the lesson.

Gallant looked over at the pea plants. "The peas could be picked in a couple weeks," Gallant said, "and there will be more peas to pick all summer long."

Sir Francis looked pleased. "How do you know?" he asked.

Gallant stepped over to one of the plants and pointed to the pods. "See? There are different sizes of pods on each plant. Some will be ready in a couple weeks, some are just getting started in growing. If the plant produces them at different stages now, it should do the same all summer."

"Well done," called out Sir Francis. "What else?"

Gallant reached down and touched a green plant with a noticeable network of veins running through its leaves. He crushed a leaf between his fingers and smelled the fragrance of the plant. "Mint!" he called out **triumphantly.**

Sir Francis looked unimpressed. "What about it, Master Gallant?"

Gallant looked back at the mint plant and noticed the edge of a wooden bucket sunken in the ground around the plant. Gallant responded: "The mint plant had been placed inside a bucket, and the bucket has been buried in the ground."

He stood up and smiled broadly, but Sir Francis was not easily impressed.

"Why would your mother do such a thing?"

Gallant thought for a minute—then he blurted out the only thing that made sense to him: "Mother said the mint plant spreads quickly; um, the bucket keeps it from overgrowing into the other plants?"

Sir Francis nodded. "Indeed. Those were all very straightforward. Let's try something a little more challenging." Gallant winced. He thought he was doing quite well. Gallant followed as Sir Francis stepped over several rows of plants and waved his hand toward a patch of carrots near a **hedge.** The bushes of the hedge were an easy marker for the edge of the garden. Closest to the hedge, the carrot greens growing above the soil were much smaller than the carrots growing four rows away.

"Why are these carrot plants so much smaller, Gallant?" Sir Francis asked. "They were all planted at the same time."

Gallant came nearer to the plants and studied them carefully. He worked through the question out loud. "They are in the same soil, they are all watered equally." Gallant was perplexed. *What could have caused these to be so stunted?* Suddenly the sun emerged from behind a cloud and Gallant noticed the hedge was casting a shadow on the ground, almost exactly in the shape of the smaller plants. "So!" he called out excitedly, "It is the sun! These plants do not have the benefit of a full day's sunlight." Gallant folded his arms and nodded, quite proud of himself.

Sir Francis nodded. "It's true." His expression turned serious. "Do you understand what you have already learned today, Gallant?"

Gallant squinted in the sunlight, which was now rising just over the knight's shoulder. "Yes, sir. I can learn even when no one is speaking."

"Correct," said Sir Francis. "Listen twice as much as you talk, Gallant. And always keep your eyes open, to learn by observing." Sir Francis handed Gallant a **hoe** and a wooden bucket. "Once you've cleared the garden of all the weeds, we will continue our class." Gallant was eager for the official lessons to begin, so he took the hoe and the bucket and walked toward the far end of the garden to begin his assignment. Before Sir Francis headed to the classroom, he reminded Gallant: "How well you accomplish small deeds will tell me how well you will accomplish large ones."

Gallant nodded and put his hoe to the ground. *How can I bring prayer into this task?* He decided on a plan: each time he finished hoeing one row and moved on to a new section of the garden, he thanked God for a different blessing. "I thank you Lord for my family," he said as he worked the ground around the carrots. He approached the onions. "Our farm." Then to the peas. "The sunshine." As he worked, he voiced his gratitude for the rain, and for their animals, and castles, armor, and knights. He especially remembered Sir Francis. Gallant ran out of vegetable rows before he ran out of the things that made him feel grateful. He set down the hoe and picked up the bucket, walking through the garden and collecting the weed piles he had created. He shook the weeds one last time, keeping as much of the precious soil in the garden as he could; and then he pressed the bunches of weeds firmly into the bucket. The more he could fit in the bucket, the fewer trips he would need to make. *You fellows won't ever be back again to clutter up our garden!* He dumped the weeds at the far end of the garden, in an area away from the plants.

It was at the half-point to the noon hour when Gallant finished clearing all the weeds from the garden. He stood a moment, resting as he leaned on the hoe. Sir Francis had once brought water for him to drink as he worked, but most of the time, Sir Francis was in the storeroom, out of the boy's sight.

Gallant took a few moments to walk the rows of vegetables to double-check that he hadn't missed any spots. *Sir Francis is testing me right now. He is waiting to see how quickly I will finish and how well I do the work when he is not watching me.* Gallant made up his mind that he would be thorough, even if doing the job perfectly took more time and more effort. *I don't want Sir Francis to be disappointed with my work.* When he was absolutely sure the task was complete, he knocked on the storeroom door before entering. Sir Francis was sitting at his table, reading a worn-looking book.

"Excuse me, sir." Gallant waited for Sir Francis to look up before he announced, "I finished my assignment."

Sir Francis kissed the page he had been reading, a sign of respect for the words of the book, then closed the book and set it squarely on the table. He joined Gallant at the door. The two walked together from the storeroom to the garden. Neither spoke. Gallant was anxious for his teacher to see how carefully he had weeded.

The knight approached the garden and stopped. He looked one way down the rows and then the other. He stepped over a few rows and looked both ways again. And then he turned to Gallant. "You have done exactly what I asked—and you have done it well."

Gallant beamed.

Sir Francis reached for Gallant's hoe and bucket. "Do you feel the satisfaction? That sense of accomplishment in knowing you have done this task well?"

"Yes, sir. I feel it." Gallant responded.

"Remember that feeling and do not settle for anything less, on any task, at any time," Sir Francis instructed. "In this way, you will never be disappointed in yourself because you will have always given your best effort."

Gallant nodded.

"So," continued the teacher, "let us begin our class." Sir Francis set the hoe and bucket aside and Gallant sat down at Sir Francis' feet, in between the rows of plants. "Plants are alive," Sir Francis started. "We eat and drink and breathe, and they eat and drink and breathe, but in a way far different."

Gallant was confused. "But they have no mouth to eat with, Sir Francis. And they have no nose to breathe."

Sir Francis responded: "They have roots growing deep into the soil. From the soil the plants draw the **nutrients** and moisture they need." Sir Francis knelt and dug gently around a plant near Gallant. It was the plant Gallant had wondered about. He knew his mother used it in her stews, but he hadn't been able to figure out what it was. As Sir Francis carefully brushed away the soil from the root of the plant, he revealed a small maroon-colored bulb.

Of course, Gallant sighed, *it's a red beet.* He shook his head for having forgotten such an easy plant. Beneath the bulb, Sir Francis revealed a tuft of fine tendrils growing out from a center root. He continued his lesson. "Through these roots, the beet collects the water and the food it needs to survive and to grow. If you cut off the roots, you stop the flow of water and nutrients to the leaves and the plant will die." Sir Francis signaled for Gallant to reach over and touch the roots.

They were soft and flexible. Sir Francis covered the roots with the rich black soil, pressing it down to be sure it was firm around the plant.

He spoke as he worked. "Since the beet takes its nutrition from the soil, the soil must be in contact with the roots. The best way to do that is to pack the soil down tightly and then to water the area thoroughly. The water will cause any gaps in the soil to fill with the dirt above. It will cause everything to settle." After Sir Francis finished moving the dirt back, he signaled to Gallant to fetch the water bucket and water the area.

Gallant poured the water as Sir Francis continued his instruction. "So plants need soil, sunlight, water, and nutrients. You must understand what time of year to plant each crop, what kind of care they require, and when to harvest them." Gallant always knew the garden was necessary and important. He was beginning to understand how much effort went into keeping it healthy. He also realized how fortunate he and his family were to live on **arable** land.

"Today we have a guest teacher, Gallant," Sir Francis announced as he stood.

Gallant's heart leapt. *A knight, I just know it. Here to share the story of his most dangerous quest!* Just then, Catherine came across the field from their home, carrying a basket in one hand and a flask of water in the other.

"My mother?" Gallant asked, looking skeptically at Sir Francis.

Sir Francis responded. "Your mother can teach you everything you need to know about keeping a garden. You will work with her today for two hours, and she will grade your effort." Gallant perked up when he realized he would be graded for his work. Sir Francis continued: "Your mother will assign you one gardening task which you will incorporate into your daily chores. Discipline always produces a fruitful harvest."

Sir Francis bowed to Gallant's mother. "God save you, Lady Catherine." He headed back to the storeroom, but after a few steps, he stopped and turned back to them both. "Now that I know you can be trusted in your work, Master Gallant, you will be considered for more important tasks."

Catherine handed her son the flask of water as she began to walk the rows of plants, looking for ripe vegetables that could be harvested. As she walked, she sang:

> *She considered a field, and bought it:*
> *with the fruit of her hands she planted...*

Think About This

1. Why does a knight have to learn how to plant a garden?

2. What was the lesson Gallant learned in the garden?

Word Helper

tilled (sounds like **till**-d): a verb, to turn over soil, to prepare it for planting

observations (sounds like ob-ser-**vay**-shons): a noun, information learned by watching something

triumphantly (sounds like try-**um**-fant-lee): an adverb, acting with joy and pride

hedge (sounds like **hej**): a noun, a row of thick shrubs that forms a kind of wall

hoe (sounds like **ho**): a noun, a tool used in the garden to scrape away weeds

nutrients (sounds like **new**-tree-ints): a noun, healthy substances

arable (sounds like **air**-uh-ball): an adjective, suitable for growing crops

If you have the Sir Gallant Castle Kit, go to your Workbook now and complete the next lesson, called Banner 5.

CHAPTER SIX

Buckets and Embers

Twice a week, for four weeks, Gallant finished his daily garden task with care and arrived early to school. Each time, he set a clean slate board on the table before him and he sat up straight to wait for Sir Francis to arrive. Gallant learned to recognize the pattern of sounds that heralded the arrival of his teacher: the horse's hooves on the ground, the squeak of the saddle as Sir Francis dismounted, the foot-steps to the door. When Gallant heard the wooden door swing open, he leapt to his feet. As Sir Francis passed him, he bowed and greeted him. "Good morning, Sir Francis."

Sir Francis always responded: "Good morning, Master Gallant."

Once Sir Francis arrived at his lectern, Gallant took his seat. So far, the knight hadn't mentioned Gallant's heart and what was written on it. Every day that passed without a mention of this made Gallant feel a bit more at ease during class. He had already made up his mind to tell his father about what he had done. *I will. I just need to decide how to do it. And when.*

Sir Francis was a scholar, a highly educated man who spent his days reading books and conversing with learned men. Gallant knew the title "Sir" meant Sir Francis was a knight, even though he didn't wear a suit of armor and carry a long sword every day. Gallant was eager to hear the story of how Sir Francis was trained and when he received his knighthood, but his father had reminded him not to ask too many questions.

Sir Francis normally wore pleated velvet coats with large **elaborate** sleeves, breeches made of finely woven linen and tall colorful socks. His clothing was coordinated in color, an indication of his high status in society. As soon as Sir Francis entered the storeroom, he lifted his hat from his head and placed it on a hook on the wall. The round hat was made of stiff felted brown wool, with a wide brim folded up all around it and a white feather jutting out from one side. Sir Francis began class with his usual prayer: "May the Good Lord bless our efforts and pour His Wisdom upon us as we seek to please Him by our studies."

Gallant responded "Amen," and then waited as Sir Francis unpacked the lesson materials from his satchel.

Sir Francis didn't talk unnecessarily. During short school breaks, he often sat quietly under a tree, lost in thought. Sir Francis was stern, but Gallant could sense his kindness. Even when Gallant was scolded, he understood Sir Francis was correcting him to help him become a better knight.

"Do you mean to train yourself to **slouch** or to write in a sloppy manner?" Sir Francis had once asked him. "Each time you do these things, you reinforce a habit that will be difficult to break."

Gallant intended to form good habits. *I must learn to do things correctly, now, while I am still young, if I am to become a proper knight when I get older.*

As today's lesson began, Gallant had been instructed to print his letters as neatly as he could. Sir Francis was very clear about the lesson:

"Take your time and print with great care, as though your slate is a work of art to be sold in the marketplace." Gallant was about half of the way through the alphabet when a noise in the distance jolted him. DONG. His chalk slipped and the letter "O" turned into a "Q." DONG. DONG. The sound of a bell came from outside, some distance away, but it was still loud and **persistent**. Sir Francis hurried to the door. He called out behind him, "Class dismissed. Go home!"

DONG. DONG.

Gallant quickly gathered his belongings and rushed out the door. Sir Francis was already on his horse, galloping away toward the town. DONG. DONG. The bell continued clanging as Gallant rushed home. He found his mother standing near the open door, with Margaret and Timothy clinging to her skirt, crying. Gallant could see the worry in his mother's face. "What is it, mother?" Gallant gasped, out of breath from running.

DONG. Catherine pulled Gallant and the other two children close to her and hugged them all tightly. "It's the town bell, Gallant. Something is wrong. The bell is calling the men to come help."

DONG. DONG.

While she was still speaking, William rushed toward the house. "Riders came to call all able-bodied men. I met one in the field," he explained. "The bakery's on fire!"

DONG.

Catherine inhaled sharply, then turned to Gallant and instructed him, "Run and collect as many empty buckets as you can find. Bring them to the wagon."

DONG. DONG.

Gallant dropped his slate board and ran while William hitched the horse onto the wagon. Catherine disappeared into the kitchen, returning with a jug of water and a small linen bag tied with string. She placed them in the wagon. Gallant reappeared with two buckets from the storeroom and one from the stable and loaded them onto the wagon bed. William leapt aboard and gathered the reins.

Gallant ran to the side of the wagon and cried out: "Father, I want to help!"

William looked at Catherine, who nodded her approval. "Climb up! Hurry!" he ordered. Gallant mounted the seat next to his father just as the horse began to move. "May the Lord grant us swift passage." William prayed as he snapped the reins.

"Be careful," Catherine called after them. She kissed her fingers and waved goodbye.

Gallant had only heard the town bell ring for joyful events, festivals and the opening of markets. The **cadence** of the bell for those celebrations was far different from the warning sound he was hearing now. Father snapped the reins again and the horse began to trot. After they left their farm, they saw men and boys hurrying to town on horseback and on foot, young men and old.

William slowed the horse several times, so those on foot could jump onto the wagon. He looked over his shoulder to be sure the riders were safely onboard, and then he focused on driving the wagon as fast as possible, straight into town. As they followed the worn, bumpy path through the fields, William told his son, "The bell signals the men to come to help. Usually no one knows what is happening until they arrive in the town square and see for themselves. If I hadn't known it was a fire, I would have grabbed a weapon before we left home. The last time the bell rang like this, the men were needed to capture a wretched criminal who had attacked the watchman and escaped."

Even before the wagon pulled up to the town square, Gallant could smell the distinct odor of a fire. Smoke was rising in plumes, then dispersing as the wind carried it away. As they got closer to the site of the bakery, he saw the flames licking up toward the sky. **Embers** danced in the air and floated on the breeze until the red glow faded. The sooner the men could extinguish the fire, the less chance an ember would float to another building and catch fire. Already a line of men had formed from the town well to the bakery. They filled buckets with water and passed them from one person to the next, all the way down the line to the fire. The strongest men were at the bakery, hurling the water onto the flames.

"Whoa! Whoa!" William called to his horse. Those who had climbed aboard the wagon leapt off and ran to the line of firefighters. William jumped from the wagon, grabbed the buckets, and quickly set them at the base of the well before he joined the line.

Sir Francis was directing the volunteers as they passed the buckets of water swiftly toward the fire. When he saw Gallant in the wagon, he called out urgently: "Gallant, take the empty buckets from the end of the water line and return them to the well!"

For a brief moment, Gallant sat frozen in place in the wagon. Men were yelling to one another as smoke billowed back and forth with the wind. It was a frightful sight for a young boy. A large cloud of smoke passed in front of Gallant and when it cleared, he saw his father at the front of the line, tossing buckets of water at the flames. *Father is so close to the flames and he's not scared. I can help too.* Gallant hopped down and ran to the area where the empty buckets had been tossed. As he approached, the heat stung his skin and dried his eyes. He squinted, holding his forearm up to shield his face. When he got to the buckets, he grabbed two large ones in each hand and spun around, his back to the fire. Just then William nodded at him, and in that glance Gallant felt the pride of a father for his courageous son. It strengthened him. Gallant rushed back to the well with the buckets, dropped them, and ran back to carry more.

Another young boy Gallant's age had been watching. He joined Gallant at the well. "Kin I hep ye?" he asked.

Gallant felt he had been assigned a very important part in trying to save the bakery, and now it was his responsibility to help train the others. "Like this!" Gallant waved for the boy to follow him. The two ran toward the fire and collected more buckets, then hurried back to the well. Both boys were breathless with excitement. This was the closest they had ever been to danger, but the fact that they were helping meant they weren't scared. The boys made two dozen trips before they got tired and started to slow down.

At first it didn't look like the water was helping at all, but then Gallant noticed the flames were smaller. Everything happened fast—no more than a third of an hour. After the flames flickered out, the men continued to throw water on the building to prevent the flames from starting up again. One man stirred the ashes on the ground with a broomstick handle while other men continued pouring buckets of water onto the blackened mess. It was a **monumental** task, but at the end of it, half the bakery building was saved. Best of all, no one was hurt and the fire did not spread.

Some firefighters were coughing from the smoke, and several were singed by the fire, but no one had sustained serious burns. Almost everybody was covered with black soot, including Gallant, but he wasn't in a hurry to clean up. The soot was a sign he had helped and he was proud to have the evidence all over his face. When the rush was over, the men and boys sat under the trees and rested while the women of the town brought them water from the well and snacks from their homes.

The two boys stood next to each other, panting, still holding their empty buckets. "Hare naw. Yon'd be da ferst fire ah ere hepped ta douse." the boy said excitedly. "Just ye wait; next time ah'l be at da front o' da line, lobbin' full buckets o' water at da flame!" the boy said excitedly.

Gallant turned to his helper and saw that his face was splashed with freckles and his hair was a wild bush of bright orange-red. In all the excitement, he hadn't really noticed before. *By his talk and by his look, he's not from around here.* The boy spoke as though his words were strung along a melody. Gallant remembered an old man in the village once said that the red-haired were fiery and bold because their ancestors had lived on the mountaintops, near to the sun. Could it be true?

"Are you from the mountains?" Gallant asked, testing the old man's theory.

"Aye. Am fae Inverlochy, near th' Ben, ta be sure. Tho ah dinnae climb to da tip-top. Why 'er would ah? There'd be nought up dare but stone as far as ye could see." he said with a smile.

"Hmm. I think you said you live near a mountain, but you had no reason to climb it." Gallant said nervously.

"Aye!" the boy replied cheerily.

"Well, no matter. I'm Gallant, what's your name?"

The boy set down the buckets. "Ma given name's Hamish, but ah go by James," he said. "We come lass nit and we'll be leavin' latur today fer Thornbury Castle," he responded. "Muh fatha's ta be the Duke's carpenter. Meh'be ahl see ye thar one day. Bye fer noo!" He disappeared into the crowd that had gathered to survey the damage to the bakery.

Gallant found his father resting near their wagon. "What caused the fire, Father?" he asked. His father nodded toward Master Clove, who was about thirty paces away, busy thanking his neighbors for their help.

"He must have swept up a hot ember without realizing it. After tidying the shop, he left to deliver a few loaves to the inn and when he returned, the fire was **raging**."

Gallant studied Master Clove. He carried extra weight at his belly, which he often and eagerly blamed on his delicious assortment of sweet fruit pies. He always wore an apron to cover his tunic and he kept his shirt sleeves rolled back, so all that Gallant usually saw were his baggy tan britches and those peculiar pointed shoes that turned upward at the toes. Master Clove once told Margaret the shoes made him run faster when he was delivering his muffins. Now his apron and sleeves were covered with black soot and his face was flushed and sweaty. His white hair told Gallant he had lived more years than Gallant's father; but the soot trapped in the lines on his face made him look far older, and very tired.

Gallant noticed that even after losing half his shop, Master Clove was smiling. *It must be because he was so grateful for all the help. Lord, please bless him as he recovers from this fright.* Master Clove found William sitting on the ground, leaning against the wagon, and he knelt down next to him to thank him warmly. The **acrid** smell of smoke clung stubbornly to his clothing and filled the air around him. "The Lord gave, and the Lord hath taken away: as it hath pleased the Lord so is it done," Master Clove said solemnly.

"Blessed be the name of the Lord," William responded. With an encouraging voice, he added: "You know how the story of Job ends! Pick the day for rebuilding and we'll be there. And tonight, we will be offering our family prayers for your needs."

Master Clove nodded, his eyes moist with tears. He stood and faced Gallant. "Your father is a good man, son." Then the baker added with a smile, "And you've obviously learned from him. Thank you, lad, for all your help today!"

After Master Clove walked away, Gallant handed his father the jug of water his mother had sent along with them. "Was Job the man in the Bible who lost his family and farm and was covered with sores, Father?"

"Yes. Through the pain and suffering he never cursed God. And because of his faithfulness, everything he lost—and more, was restored back to him." William watched Master Clove move on to thank another group of men. "This is what it means to love your neighbor, Gallant," William said. "We care for one other, laboring as if all things depend on us; and praying as if all things depend on God." And even though Gallant hadn't been at school for very long that day, he knew he had just learned a very valuable lesson.

Gallant climbed into the wagon and retrieved the linen pouch his mother had sent along. He gave it to his father, who untied the string and peeled back the fabric. William took a few nuts and then reached over and offered them to Gallant. They were almonds, his favorite. The two shared their refreshing snack and watched as people bustled about the town square. Off in the distance, Gallant heard the distinctive clanging of a hammer against metal. Most likely, the blacksmith had returned to his shop and was now hammering a tool of some sort, but Gallant imagined he was pounding out the breastplate for a new suit of armor.

"Father? In class today, I was told to practice my writing. After so many classes, I've still not seen helmet nor **gauntlet**." Gallant said mournfully.

"Hold your peace and do not presume to instruct your tutor," his father advised. "Your task now is to be attentive and obedient."

Gallant knew by the tone of his father's voice that the discussion was over, but he was beginning to wonder if Sir Francis intended to teach him knight things at all.

Think About This

1. What lesson did Gallant learn at the fire? (HINT: It's something Gallant's father told him after they put out the fire).

2. A civil servant is a person whose job helps a community of people. They are paid by the tax money collected from all the citizens, because the work of the civil servant supports everyone in the city, state or country. A firefighter is a civil servant. What do the firefighters do for your community? Nowadays, they don't just put out fires. If you don't know, ask one!

Memory Test

What were the three lessons Gallant learned on his first day of school? Try to remember without looking, but if you have to look, write the lessons down. Writing things helps you remember them.

Word Helper

elaborate (sounds like ee-**lab**-oar-it): an adjective, fancy or decorated

slouch (sounds like **slauwch**): a verb, to slump, as in a chair, not to sit up straight

persistent (sounds like purr-**sis**-tent): an adjective, something that continues to happen

cadence (sounds like **kay**-dense): a noun, the beat or pattern of a sound

embers (sounds like **em**-burr): a noun, small burning pieces of wood or coal from a fire

monumental (sounds like mon-you-**men**-tall): adjective, very large or prominent

raging (sounds like **ray**-jing): verb, with violent action

acrid (sounds like **ack**-rid): an adjective, bitter, unpleasant

gauntlet (sounds like **gawnt**-let): a noun, a glove
made of metal

If you have the Sir Gallant Castle Kit, go to
your Workbook now and complete the next
lesson, called Banner 6.

CHAPTER SEVEN

Wilderness Classroom

Gallant was never again late for school. Ever since the first day when he missed the greatest lesson of knighthood, he always made sure he was sitting at his desk when Sir Francis entered the storeroom. But one day, the teacher arrived before the student. Gallant found Sir Francis waiting outside—and he was not dressed like a schoolteacher, he was dressed like a farmer who was going to work in the field. A full water flask hung over his shoulder and a five-inch leather sheath was tied to his belt with leather strips, the wooden handle of a knife protruding above the covered blade. Gallant wasn't sure what this meant, but he knew it had something to do with the lesson for the day. *How exciting!*

"Gallant," Sir Francis called, "place your slate in the storeroom. We will be taking our lesson outside today." The morning was warm and sunny, but windy enough to cause the white puffs of seedlings to float on the breeze. The coordinated whine of the insects signaled high summer. *Finally! Surely we will practice sword-fighting. We need the large open field to swing the weapons freely.* But as soon as Gallant placed his slate in the storeroom and stepped back outside, Sir Francis jogged away from the storehouse, into the woods. "We're going for a little run, Gallant," he shouted over his shoulder. "Keep up with me. And may the Good Lord bless our efforts and pour His Wisdom upon us as we seek to please Him by our studies."

"Amen," responded Gallant, but by the time he started after Sir Francis, he was already ten paces behind. He quickly learned that Sir Francis was a swift runner. Gallant sprinted to catch up, but the effort winded him, and he struggled to steady his breathing.

The two ran past William and Catherine's property line and into a wooded area full of new saplings. The ground rose and fell, mainly covered with greenery, but occasionally dotted with rocks, which they had to dodge. Gallant watched the ground closely, careful not to step on any stones. Spraining an ankle in the wilderness would cause a real hardship; especially far away from the farm, with no nearby wagon or horse. Still, they ran. Gallant wasn't used to this kind of exercise and he was quickly tiring.

Sir Francis was a skilled runner, darting in between trees and hopping over small tributaries of water. Gallant grew more fatigued and now his teacher was ten paces ahead. He glanced back to check the boy's progress, but he didn't slow down. Gallant lost track of the time, but he thought they must have been running for nearly an hour by now. His breathing grew raspy and shallow. Never had he run this far or for this long. His legs were **wobbly**, and his mouth was dry. *Oh, if only I had a cup of water.* But thinking about water made him slow down even more.

Sir Francis called to him from fifteen paces away. "Gallant, do you want to be a knight?"

Gallant perked up. He forgot about the cup of water. He forgot about his dry mouth and his wobbly legs. He even forgot to worry about the sound of his breathing. "Yes, sir," he said between big gulps of air.

"Well, then you must catch up to me. I am about to tell you the first **principle** of being a knight."

At last! The knight's promise inspired Gallant and he was infused with a **burst** of energy. He sprinted until he was running alongside Sir Francis. Together, the two of them jumped a log that five minutes earlier Gallant would have stopped to climb over. *I can't believe I did that!*

"What were you thinking about as you started to lag behind me?" Sir Francis asked as they continued to run, now side by side.

Gallant was embarrassed to answer. "I was thinking about (huff) how tired I was (huff) and how thirsty." Gallant knew that wasn't what Sir Francis wanted to hear, but it was the truth. And if there was one thing Gallant knew, it was to always tell the truth, because knights do not lie.

Together, they started down a hill. If he wasn't careful, Gallant's tired legs might not keep up with the inertia of his body falling forward. Tripping now would send Gallant sprawling onto a bed of pebbles; and considering how they crunched under the runners' feet, some were sharp enough to cut through the boy's clothing. Gallant refused to be distracted by the danger. *I missed my very first lesson, the one about the quickest and surest way to become a knight. I must not miss this one.* Gallant kept pace with Sir Francis.

"The first principle to being a good knight is that you must stay focused," Sir Francis announced. As he spoke, Gallant noticed that despite all the running, the knight wasn't even breathing hard. "When you are focused on your mission, you are better able to complete it," the teacher said. Gallant tried to focus on the running because that was his mission at the moment.

"As soon as your mind starts to wander, you lose focus, Gallant."

As they passed through a meadow of wild-flowers, Gallant stayed focused and the two ran side by side. Gallant was gasping and panting as he ran, and he could feel his heart thumping wildly. Sir Francis didn't notice, although the sound was very loud to Gallant. After a few minutes, Gallant remembered how tired he was and his pace slowed. He imagined a cool bucket of water was being poured over his head. In his mind, he lapped up the crisp freshness as it drained past his mouth. *Oh, for some water!*

Gallant dropped five steps behind Sir Francis. Then ten steps behind.

Sir Francis called out to Gallant: "Do you see the big oak tree on the crest of the hill?"

Gallant gasped, "Yes, (huff) I (puff) see it."

Sir Francis waved Gallant on. "Focus. We will run to that tree."

That tree is not so very far away. No more than fifty paces, to be sure. The meadow sloped gently upward toward the tree and Gallant already knew that the short wildflowers were easy to run through. He pushed himself harder and caught up to Sir Francis.

"I (huff) can do it, (puff) Sir Francis, (puff) I can make it to the (huff) tree." Gallant remained alongside Sir Francis until they neared the tree; then he slowed down, **anticipating** their rest.

But once again, Sir Francis pointed ahead. "Do you see the fence post just across the trail? Through the opening in those trees? We will run to that fence post."

When he realized they weren't going to stop immediately, Gallant tripped and nearly fell, his arms flailing wildly until he had regained his balance. He looked in the direction Sir Francis was pointing. The fence post was another fifty paces further. *I can do this.* Gallant continued to run. *Forget how thirsty you are, Gallant, focus on the fence post.* Salty sweat dripped into Gallant's eyes as he wiped his forehead with his sleeve. *Forget your stinging eyes. Forget how fast your heart is beating, focus. Focus on the fence post.* The two ran side by side until at last they reached the post.

When they arrived, Sir Francis slowed to a walk. Gallant sighed with relief. Groaning, he dropped onto the ground, pulling in big gulps of air. Sir Francis stopped and called out to him sharply: "On your feet, Gallant. A knight does not reveal his limits, otherwise the enemy will simply wait for him to tire."

Gallant hurried in his effort to stand, but his legs were shaky and weak. He walked stiffly next to Sir Francis, taking large breaths with each step, surprised he could learn about knighthood even in times of rest and recovery. Once their breathing slowed, Sir Francis stopped, pulled the strap of his animal-skin flask over his head, removed the leather-covered wooden stopper, and offered Gallant a drink. The boy slurped the pomegranate juice eagerly, trying not to take too much, but desperate to quench his thirst. He returned the flask to Sir Francis, who held the flask but didn't drink.

"Why did you stumble after we reached the big tree?" Sir Francis asked, eyeing the flask in his hand. Before Gallant could respond, Sir Francis answered the question for him. "You stumbled because you set the tree as your limit. You told yourself it was as far as you needed to go. So, when you reached it, you expected to stop." Gallant winced. He knew Sir Francis was right. The knight continued, "Then, when I directed you to the fence post, that became your limit. Do you see? The tree was not your limit at all, the boundary was just in your mind. If I had pointed out another landmark after the fence post, I **daresay** you would have found the strength to reach it. You must fight to overcome the limits you set for yourself, Gallant, if you are to become a knight."

Sir Francis plugged the flask and swung the strap over his shoulder.

"You didn't even take a drink!" Gallant observed the sweat that drenched the knight's tunic at his chest and under his arms. "Aren't you thirsty?"

"I am quite thirsty, but delaying the things I want most teaches me to be master over them, instead of being in bondage to them. Gallant, you must learn that some things are more important than your comfort."

Sir Francis looked around the open field where they stood. Thick forested patches surrounded them. "Now, then, which way is home, Gallant?"

The boy wheeled around, realizing that nothing looked familiar to him. He had been so busy trying to keep up with Sir Francis that he had not observed any landmarks along the way. *I know better than to get lost in the forest!* Gallant looked back and forth several times before he was forced to admit that he did not know his way back to the farm. "I—I don't know, sir." Embarrassed, Gallant looked up at the sky. The sun was no longer overhead; they were past high noon. But knowing which way was east wasn't going to help him now; he had not paid attention to the position of the sun as they ran. Once they had left his farm, he was distracted by his exhaustion and even forgot to memorize natural markers along the way, such as large trees, animal paths, or groves of unique shrubs or flowers.

"Well," Sir Francis said slowly, "suppose we had to stay the night right here. What's the first thing we do?"

"Start a fire." Gallant knew that he could scrounge for nuts or fruits to keep up his energy, but he could not survive a chilly night without heat. And it was a challenge to find the right supplies to make a fire once it was dark. Besides that, the smoke from a fire might draw the attention of a passing villager or local farmer who could help him get home.

"Find the drill wood and the kindling, Gallant," Sir Francis ordered. "I'll collect firewood and find a suitable base board." Gallant ran to the edge of the tree line, skimming the ground for the perfect stick. He needed a dry one as long as his arm and as thick as his pointer finger, with a soft center. He picked several off the ground and tossed them away before he found the perfect branch. Then he gathered two handfuls of dry twigs and leaves and brought them back to Sir Francis.

Sir Francis had carved a circle into the ground with the heel of his shoe and was laying the last few stones to line the fire pit, which was about two feet across, from stone to stone. Each stone was about the size of a small melon. Sir Francis situated the ring next to a fallen log that would serve as a place to sit, as well as a screen to block the wind from extinguishing the flame. The exposed dirt around the stones would keep the fire from spreading into the meadow grass, while the stones rimming the fire would absorb the heat and prevent the fire from igniting nearby brush.

Gallant observed a pile of dry twigs in the center of the fire pit. He set his kindling gently on top and waited. When Sir Francis finished stacking the wood he had collected, the boy handed the drill stick to him. The knight studied the branch and then pulled his knife and removed the smaller branches by shaving them off.

"This is a good choice, Gallant," he said. "The tapered base and the wider top allows you to spin the drill faster. It's nearly straight, which gives you the advantage of conserving your energy as you work the stick. Your father has taught you well." He handed the drill stick back to Gallant, who grinned at the unexpected praise.

The stick was meant to drill down into a flat board. The **friction** of the two pieces of wood rubbing together would create heated sawdust which could then be blown into flame on the dry leaves. Sir Francis cut a rounded depression out of the flat board, placing the smaller tip of the drill stick into it a couple times until the hole was just large enough to allow the drill to spin. Then he placed the flat board on the ground next to the fire pit and knelt on one knee, holding the board steady with his other foot.

Gallant knelt next to Sir Francis and placed the smaller end of the drill stick into the cut area of the flat board. He grasped the top of the drill stick, as though he were clapping, with the stick running between his hands. Then he moved his hands back and forth in opposite directions, causing the drill stick to spin. The faster he moved his hands, the faster the drill spun into the flat board. One minute passed, two, three. Gallant continued to spin, trying to ignore the drips of perspiration forming on his forehead. A few minutes later, a tiny wisp of smoke rose from the area where the drill was spinning on the flat board. Gallant continued to spin. More smoke streamed out. Still, he spun the drill furiously. His hands were sore from the stick and he was breathing heavily.

"That should do." Sir Francis said. Gallant pulled the drill away, dropped the drill stick, and focused on the flat board. A small patch of sawdust, no bigger than the tip of Gallant's thumb, remained in the depression on the flat board. Gallant blew on it just slightly, and it began to glow. He grabbed a small handful of the dried leaves and held them over the burning ember until the entire batch began to smoke heavily. Then he gently turned the steaming debris over into the fire pit, allowing the sawdust ember to settle into the waiting kindling. Gallant continued to blow on it. It took practice to know how to breathe over the smoking pile so that the emerging flame was fed, but not extinguished. Within seconds, a small flame leapt into view, then another.

Once the flames started, Gallant added larger and larger twigs until the fire was strong enough to take small logs. At long last, the fire was established. Gallant sat back and rested, drawing long, deep breaths. Starting a fire took a lot of energy.

"Now, what food have we?" Sir Francis asked.

"I saw some gooseberries while I was looking for the drill stick. They're still green, but large enough to pick. I'll gather some." Gallant stood and pulled his shirt out from under his belt and held it up from the bottom edge to use as a container for the berries.

Sir Francis surveyed the field around them. "Surely there must be some **filberts** growing

nearby. I mean to find some nut-laden shrubs."
He headed off in the opposite direction. The two
met back again at the fire after about three quarters
of an hour, each carrying a hearty batch of their
findings; and together they sat on the log near the
fire. After Sir Francis led them in prayer, they
shared their meal. Sir Francis opened his flask
and offered Gallant another drink. This time,
Gallant waited.

"After you, sir." Sir Francis nodded and took
a drink, then passed the flask to Gallant. Gallant
paused before he drank, remembering Sir Francis'
words about delaying things that he most wanted.

The knight and the boy sat at the fire, silently
watching the flames leap and vanish. Gallant
remembered the bakery fire and realized how fire
was both critical for their survival and yet also
life-threatening. It required careful handling and
respect. He considered the lessons he had learned
helping to put out the flames; and then it occurred
to him that he was learning still.

"We're not really lost, are we?" Gallant
finally said, looking up at Sir Francis as they sat
side by side on the log.

Sir Francis smiled. "No, we're not. But then,
I never said we were."

This, too, was a part of his training, a test to see how well he could manage if he were stranded alone in an unfamiliar place. Gallant hoped he had passed the test.

"You did well, lad." And with that, Sir Francis began the story about the day his father had run with him into the forest—"You see, I was given this very same test," he told his student, "when I was not much older than you are. But the day had been far colder and the cloak I wore was not sufficient against the chill. Even the fire wasn't enough to **stave** off the frigid air."

"What did you do to survive?" Gallant asked.

"My father cut his own cloak in two and gave me half. I never forgot his example. When we returned home," Sir Francis concluded, "my father gave me the other half of the cloak. I often wear it, still bearing the mark of the cut; sewn back together by the castle's seamstress, as a reminder of that lesson and my father's love and generosity so many years ago."

Gallant asked Sir Francis all the questions that had been bottled up inside him since they first met. They talked until dark, stopping only once to collect enough wood to last the night. Gallant knew they would be heading home in the morning and he rehearsed the story he would tell his mother and father about his adventure. He was eager tell Margaret and Timothy too, but he had to be careful not to alarm them when he mentioned the part about getting lost. *Margaret will cry if she thinks I might not have returned.* Gallant never wanted to be the source of his little sister's tears.

As he stared at the fire, he started to **formulate** what he would say, but his mind was fuzzy with sleep and his head slowly dropped forward. When his chin hit his chest, he startled himself awake and looked about. He stood and yawned a large, slow, open-mouthed stretch.

Sir Francis was sitting on the log, leaning forward with his forearms resting on his knees, thoughtful and contented. He stirred when Gallant stood, tossed a twig into the fire, and then sat upright and looked up into the dark sky, as if **savoring** the mantle of stars and the quiet of night. He looked at the boy.

"Rest, Gallant. I will keep watch until morning."

Gallant bowed to Sir Francis and wished him a pleasant sleep before he found a patch of ground near the fire to lie down. The white flowers of a

honeysuckle plant, clinging to a branch near his head, shared their sweet aroma as he drifted off to sleep.

Sir Francis spoke quietly to himself. "Today, we challenged your body. Next week, we will challenge your mind."

Think About This

1. What have you tried to do that was really difficult? Did you keep trying or did you give up?

2. Can you see how overcoming challenges can make you stronger and more confident?

Word Helper

wobbly (sounds like **wobb**-lee): an adverb, to feel shaky and faint

principle (sounds like **prin**-si-pall): a noun, an important point, a main issue

burst (sounds like **berrst**): a noun, an explosion, a sudden effort

anticipating (sounds like an-**tiss**-ih-pate-ing): a verb, to look forward to something

daresay (sounds like dair-**say**): a verb, to believe, to expect something might happen

friction (sounds like **frick**-shun): a noun, irritation or heat caused by the movement of two items in contact with each other

filberts (sounds like fill-**burtz**): a noun, a hazelnut

stave (sounds like **stave**): a verb, to keep away

formulate (sounds like **form**-you-late): a verb, to plan, to arrange something in your mind

savoring (sounds like **save**-oar-ing): a verb, relishing, enjoying something slowly

honeysuckle (sounds like **hun**-nee-**suck**-l): a noun, a sweet-smelling plant

---

If you have the Sir Gallant Castle Kit, go to your Workbook now and complete the next lesson, called Banner 7.

CHAPTER EIGHT

Ḥungry in the Woods

A week after his camping lesson, Gallant woke early, threw the covers aside and leaped out of bed. His mother had set out a breakfast of oatmeal bread with soft herb cheese for everyone. Gallant sat on the bench at the trestle table and said the quickest prayer he knew: "Thank you Lord for this food." With that, he selected a large slab of bread and took such an enormous bite that when he pulled the bread away, the soft cheese clung to his cheeks. The little ones were just starting to squeak their morning wake-up sounds. Timothy sat up and looked around the room, acquainting himself with the new day.

When he caught sight of Gallant's face smeared with cheese, he began to giggle and point, causing Margaret to pull back her blanket and stare. Soon they were both laughing heartily.

Gallant didn't mind entertaining them. He was still savoring his birthday celebration from the evening before. He pulled his shoes over to where he sat, and put them on, winking at his siblings as they laughed. Then he gathered his school supplies at the table and looked at the two with a quizzical expression. "What's so funny?" he asked, scratching his nose and his chin, deliberately avoiding the smear of cheese on either side of his face.

They laughed all the harder, Margaret pointing to her own cheeks to help Gallant identify the problem, while Timothy jumped on the bed with delight. At last, because Gallant needed to pull his tunic over his head, he wiped the cheese off his face, licking the last bits off his finger. Just about that time, the door swung open, spilling the morning light into the room. Catherine carried a basket full of fresh eggs hooked on the elbow of one arm as she picked off a few remaining chicken feathers. She set the basket beside the fire pit.

"Good morning little dears!" she called out.

"Mama!" both little ones replied in unison, as they left their bed and headed to the table.

Gallant was eager to get to school. *This is the first day I have ever worn a money bag. And not only that, but I have money in it!* He grabbed his slate and chalk, ran to kiss his mother, waved to his siblings, and then headed through the open door. He was so excited he started to skip along and sing a little tune his mother taught him the night before.

> *The porridge is hot*
> *and there's a pillow on my cot;*
> *two coins in a purse,*
> *let's have another verse!*

The song kept repeating itself, but a coin was added each time. Gallant sang his way to nine coins before he arrived at the storehouse. He took his seat and set his slate board on the table in front of him, then he reached to his waist and opened up the leather money pouch attached to his belt. It was a simple bag made of scrap deerskin, held closed with a horn-shaped wooden button. The leather cord woven through the edges kept the contents secure and the loop on the back allowed his belt to slip through, holding the money bag in place at his waist.

Gallant's father assembled the coin pouch in the evening hours, after the boy had fallen asleep. Just last night, Gallant's mother prepared a feast for his birthday dinner, and everyone sang a birthday song to Gallant. Then his father presented him with the money bag.

"It's perfect!" exclaimed Gallant. "I shall carry it always."

Margaret and Timothy jumped up and down and clapped when they saw the gift. Margaret waited on her tip-toes until she was able to hold the money pouch for a few moments. When she finally had it in her hands, she stroked the soft tanned deerskin against her cheek. While Timothy waited for his turn, he ran to his bed, crouched down and pulled out his rock collection, which he kept in the hollow of a short thick branch Gallant had found for him on their property. He selected a smooth spotted stone and ran back to the table, dropping it quickly inside Gallant's money bag and then checking twice to be sure it was still there.

Gallant liked being the big brother and he was eager to share his excitement with them both.

"Thank you Timothy! I think this is one of your best-looking stones. I will treasure it."

"Best have money in the pouch if you mean to carry it," his mother had said, then she stepped forward and handed Gallant two silver coins, a **groat** and a half-groat. *Two coins of my own!* Gallant had never seen more than one coin at a time. Most often, they purchased what they needed by trading wool, or milk or vegetables. Gallant looked at the two coins with big round eyes.

"Oh, thank you, Mother! Thank you, Father! I shall be very careful about how I spend these."

His father nodded approvingly. "It's your money, lad, so you can spend it as you like. But think carefully before you do."

Gallant understood. "I shall, Father. Perhaps I won't spend them at all. Perhaps I'll save all my coins until I have enough to buy a suit of armor!"

Gallant smiled as he remembered the festivities of the night before. He could hardly sit still in the classroom as he waited for Sir Francis. Within minutes, the large wooden door creaked open and his teacher walked into the classroom. Gallant stood quickly and bowed as Sir Francis walked past.

"Good morning, sir."

"Good morning," Sir Francis replied.

Gallant was too excited even to wait until Sir Francis had hung his hat. "Would you like to see my new money bag?" the boy asked eagerly. He wanted to run up to Sir Francis, but he had learned he must be called forward if he wished to approach the teacher during class.

"Come."

Gallant carried the coins in his hand as he removed the money bag from his belt and approached the lectern. When he reached Sir Francis, he placed the bag and the two coins carefully into Sir Francis' hand.

"So," said Sir Francis, "*two* coins. And a coin pouch to hold them, I see." Sir Francis examined the deerskin bag carefully. When he peered inside, he saw the stone that Timothy had given Gallant. He reached for it. "Another treasure?" Sir Francis asked, holding it up.

"Timothy gave me one of his favorites for my birthday."

"Well, happy birthday, lad!"

Gallant stood beaming until Sir Francis handed him back the bag, the coins and the stone and motioned for him to take his seat. Gallant slid his coins and rock into his money pouch and pulled his belt through the loop.

"May the Good Lord bless our efforts and pour His Wisdom upon us as we seek to please Him by our studies."

After the "Amen," he told Gallant, "Your new coin pouch fits with today's lesson quite well, Gallant. You are to go to market. I shall ask you to run an errand, carry a message, and bring back three items. When you return, we will work on mathematics. We will also learn how to read a scale and a measuring **ladle**." Gallant pulled out his slate board so he could record Sir Francis' order.

"No," said Sir Francis. "No slate. You must memorize what I am requesting. You will not always have a slate board to rely upon. You must train your mind to remember." Gallant set the board down and stood to take the order. "I should like one-quarter cup of **mulling spices**, one young chicken, and eight sticks of cinnamon." Gallant repeated each item slowly. *This is going to be easy.*

Sir Francis continued: "Master Wheatfield's assistant is tending my herd while I am away. You shall tell Master Wheatfield that **twoscore** of the sounder of swine are now being herded to Thornbury. One was injured and had to be put down. The rest will need feedings for the next twenty-seven days. Any that reach thirty-three stones in weight ought to be brought to market for sale."

Gallant shifted from foot to foot as a bead of sweat formed on his upper lip. *Uh-oh. Maybe this isn't going to be so easy.*

"There is a device you can use to help you remember." Sir Francis advised. "Picture yourself in a comfortable place—your home perhaps. Walk around the room and imagine each familiar item represents what you must remember. The odder the image, the more likely you will remember. Now, close your eyes." Sir Francis paused a moment. "You enter your house and a group of pigs are balanced—tail to snout—in the shape of the number forty, on top your mattress. One holds a sign with an arrow that points to Thornbury. That represents the twoscore of the sounder being herded to Thornbury. Now, in your mind, keep moving about your home. One more pig you find, injured, resting on the wooden chest. Twenty-seven bowls of acorns on your mother's loom represent the twenty-seven days of feeding. Finally, you find your money bag open on the trestle table, next to thirty-three of Timothy's rocks. The money bag reminds you that those swine weighing thirty-three stones are to be sold. Do you understand?"

Gallant opened his eyes and nodded, now more sure of himself.

Sir Francis added: "Oh, and Gallant, you may stop at the bakery and buy a cranberry roll for yourself. The stone oven survived the fire. Master Clove is baking again."

Gallant loved cranberry rolls, so he had to really concentrate on the instructions so that he didn't forget everything but the roll.

Sir Francis had one more instruction: "Tell Master Wheatfield he should keep the change and put it toward my account at the market. Now, repeat the order and the instructions."

"One-quarter cup of mulling spices, one young chicken, and eight sticks of cinnamon," recited Gallant. Sir Francis nodded, and Gallant continued, closing his eyes again to picture his home and all the images: "I must inform Master Wheatfield that twoscore of your sounder of swine are being herded to Thornbury. One was resting, uh, I mean injured, and had to be put down. Um—the remainder—the remainder will need feeding for the next twenty- uh, twenty-seven days. Any that reach thirty-three stones should be taken to market for sale. And I can buy a cranberry roll for myself."

Sir Francis handed the boy a gold coin called a sovereign, worth about 20 shillings; and shooed him on his way. Gallant started out of the storeroom at a run. He glanced at the coin as he ran, and he noticed how it glinted in the sunlight. *Real gold! Such a beautiful coin.* But there was no time to study it now. *I've got to get to the market before I forget the order.* He kept repeating the order over and over as he ran, racing along the rutted path to town for nearly two **furlongs** before he slowed down to a walk. He stopped for a moment to study the coin; observing a coat-of-arms on one side and a king seated on his throne on the other side. He balanced the gold coin on his thumb, then flipped it high, watching it spin in the air. *Someday when I am a knight, I will have many gold coins.*

Gallant began to walk again, tossing and catching the coin as he went. He passed into an area of forest covered with vibrant bluebell flowers, their trumpet-shaped pedals dangling delicately from the stems. Gallant held the coin in his fist as he stopped to admire the scene: the carpet of velvet blue contrasted with the lush vibrant green of the lower-hanging leaves. *Mother would love to see this!* It was then he noticed an elderly woman who had been crossing the path a short distance in front of him. She was bent over and held a stick to balance herself.

"Good day and God save you," Gallant called out.

The woman didn't answer, but she had stopped and was watching Gallant approach. As he neared, she called out weakly: "God save you, my boy. Can you spare something for a poor old widow who hasn't eaten in two days?"

Gallant had never been asked for food. *Father and Mother always have something to give away when they meet a beggar in the street.* He realized that the old woman must have seen him tossing a shiny gold coin, so he tried to explain his situation. "I'm sorry," Gallant opened his hand to reveal the gold coin as he spoke, "I'm on my way to the market with someone else's money. It is not mine to give." Gallant bowed and walked past the woman and down the path a distance before he remembered that he had two coins in his money bag. He immediately stopped and turned around to see if the woman was still there, but she had disappeared. *I could run after her and give her one of my coins, but I'm saving them for the suit of armor. Anyway, she's already gone.*

Gallant turned back to his path and hurried along. At the market, he remembered everything he was to purchase and he conveyed the instructions just as he had memorized them. Master Wheatfield placed the spices and the cinnamon sticks into a small burlap sack which Gallant tied to his belt, next to his money pouch. Then the shopkeeper stepped behind his store and selected a live chicken from his collection. Gallant watched through the doorway as the merchant tied a strap around the wings of the bird and knotted a string around its feet. He returned to the store and handed Gallant the bird, reminding him to carry it by its feet. Gallant kept a small copper coin for a cranberry roll and returned the rest of the change to Master Wheatfield, just as he had been instructed.

"It's to be applied to the account of Sir Francis," Gallant told him.

With the account now settled, Gallant rushed to the bakery to buy a cranberry roll. When he arrived, he noticed that two walls and the entire roof were missing, but the burned and charred timbers were gone and the ash had been swept away. The bakery building was ready for repair and stacks of roughly hewn timber lay on the ground awaiting assembly. Gallant watched Master Clove retrieve a tray of bread and rolls from the oven, using a long wooden pole to move the other items around inside the large stone enclosure. When the baker turned back around, he saw Gallant standing at the counter.

"What brings you here today, lad?" the baker asked cheerily.

"One cranberry roll, if you please, my good man!" Gallant said, quite full of himself for having money to spend. He set the copper coin on the counter, looking past the baker and eagerly eyeing the rolls. Master Clove played along, straightening up and then bowing in an exaggerated way.

"Right away, sir!" He selected the biggest roll from the batch, wrapped it in a thin cloth and handed it to Gallant. The steam was still swirling from it.

"Watch yourself, my Lord!" Master Clove warned. "Lest the heat burn your tender royal mouth." The baker winked at Gallant, who enjoyed being treated as nobility, if only for a moment. He took the roll and headed to the street. *Mmmmm. It smells wonderful.* With the roll in one hand and the chicken in the other, Gallant began the journey back to Sir Francis, humming the tune he was singing earlier.

He'd traveled just a short way when he met the old woman again. She was seated on a tree stump, not far from where he'd seen her before, her walking stick resting against her shoulder. Gallant was enjoying his first bite of the cranberry roll when he saw her. Something tugged at his heart when he remembered she said she had not eaten in two days. *I had cheese and bread this morning. Already I am better fed.* He walked straight to her and held out the roll.

"I've taken a bite, but there's still plenty left. Would you like my cranberry roll?" he asked.

The woman, who looked weary and frail, gazed at Gallant from where she sat. She answered in a voice barely more than a whisper. "Yes. Thank you." She took the roll and tore a piece from it, then chewed it slowly. "Perhaps this will be my last meal," she murmured. "I've had no flour and no salt since last week, and no crops to trade for either."

Gallant knew some people struggled for their daily food, but he had never met someone alone like this, without his mother or father to provide help. Gallant set down his chicken and reached into his coin pouch. "I think these coins would be better spent by you," he said, and he gently laid his two silver coins into the old woman's hand. Before she could say anything, Gallant picked up the chicken and ran away.

Gallant ran so the old woman wouldn't see his tears. "Knights don't cry," he reminded himself sternly. Even though he knew in his heart it was the right thing to do, he was still sad his coins were gone. But the tears soon dried, and Gallant consoled himself with the thought that the old woman would sleep well tonight. He started to smile. *She's probably at the market right now, buying flour and salt and milk. Maybe even a chicken! And tonight, she will dream happy dreams with a full stomach.*

By this time, Gallant was close to home. He had been gone for about an hour and a half, and as he neared the storeroom, he could see Sir Francis sitting on the ground, leaning against a tree and reading his favorite book.

Sir Francis heard Gallant nearing. He stood and placed his book in his satchel, then hooked his satchel strap over his shoulder. Gallant hurried to him and handed him the bird. "Your chicken, sir." He untied the burlap bag from his belt and spoke proudly as he extended the spice bag, "One quarter-cup of mulling spices and eight cinnamon sticks. Master Wheatfield received your instructions just as you conveyed them to me." Gallant bowed deeply when he finished speaking.

"And did you have any trouble along the way?" the teacher asked, as he examined the chicken.

Gallant wasn't sure if his interaction with the old woman should be called trouble. He thought a moment. "Well, not really trouble," he finally answered.

Sir Francis looked intently at him. "Tell me, Gallant. What **transpired?**"

Gallant looked toward his home. Smoke was rising from the roof vents. He and his mother had gathered vegetables from their abundant garden just last night. They were having **leek** soup for dinner. He scanned the field, where the sheep grazed on the grasses of the fertile soil and gave them milk for butter and cheese. He glanced toward the chicken coop and thought of the abundance of eggs and their occasional chicken meal. Then he focused his gaze back at Sir Francis.

"Today, Sir Francis," he said, "I learned what two silver coins can buy."

Sir Francis looked **intrigued**. "Explain." Gallant told Sir Francis about the old woman and how he had passed her up on the way to the market. Sir Francis waited patiently while Gallant finished the story. When he spoke about giving his cranberry roll and his two coins to the woman, Sir Francis rested his hand on Gallant's head. "You're a good lad, Gallant. You will make a fine knight." With those words of praise lingering in the air, Sir Francis walked to the storeroom and pulled open the door. He looked back at the boy and announced, "You've learned enough for one day. We will save our measurements and mathematics for another class." Then he tossed the small burlap sack full of spices back to Gallant. "These are for your mother. She will surely have a better recipe than I."

Gallant received the sack with great excitement. Spices were a rare treat in his house. "Thank you, Sir Francis, and God save you!" He started to skip, happy to be bringing spices home to his mother. But he was even more pleased because he had done something so well that a knight had praised him. That was the best news

Gallant could have hoped for. *So the secret in my heart doesn't mean that I am a bad boy, especially since I will never steal anything ever again. And I will make things right, by God's grace.*

Gallant felt as if a heavy wooden beam had been lifted off his shoulders. He started to sing his song as he skipped, but he changed the words just a little so that the song was now about the old woman he had met on the road:

> *The porridge is hot*
> *and there's a pillow on **her** cot;*
> *two coins in **her** purse,*
> *let's have another verse.*

Gallant couldn't wait for his next class. He was sure that Sir Francis thought well enough of him that he would soon introduce him to other knights, or maybe even take him to a jousting tournament. *Finally, finally, I am ready to learn the lessons of a knight.*

Think About This

1. Can someone be generous even without any money?

2. What would you have done if you saw the old woman in the woods?

3. Can you think of someone you would like to help?

Word Helper

porridge (sounds like **pour**-ij): a noun, a hot cereal

groat (sounds like **grote**): a noun, a coin used in England in the Middle Ages, worth about 1/3 of a shilling

ladle (sounds like **lay**-dull): a noun, a long scooped spoon used in cooking

mulling spices (sounds like **muh**-ling): a noun, a combination of dried plants that have a unique smell and taste when heated, often used to flavor food or scent the air

twoscore (sounds like too-**skor**): an adjective, equaling 40 items

stone (sounds like **stone**): a noun, a unit of weight equaling 12 pounds

furlong (sounds like **fur**-long), a noun, a unit of distance equaling one-eighth of a mile

transpired (sounds like tran-**spire**-d): a verb, occurred or happened

leek (sounds like **leek**): a noun, a vegetable similar in taste to an onion

intrigued (sounds like in-**tree**-gd): an adverb, to be interested

> If you have the Sir Gallant Castle Kit, go to your Workbook now and complete the next lesson, called Banner 8.

CHAPTER NINE
Field Trip Exam

Just when Gallant became accustomed to the routine of his school classes, Sir Francis would do something remarkable. On this particular morning, Gallant was about to leave his home for the storehouse when his mother handed him a leather flask full of water. Since they had a well on their property, Gallant knew this meant he was going to be away from home. *We must be going to the fairgrounds, to learn to joust!* His mother also handed him a loaf of fine white bread called manchet, which she wrapped in a clean linen cloth and tied with a woolen string.

"You should bring something to offer your host," she said. "Enjoy your field trip!" She kissed him on the forehead and ushered him out the door.

When Gallant arrived at the storeroom, he sat down at his usual place and waited. Within a few minutes, he heard the distinctive rhythmic stomp of horses' hooves on the ground, but the pacing indicated more than one horse; and their steps were accompanied by the squeaking sound of a wagon bumping over the field. Gallant jumped up to see whose horses and wagon were approaching. He pulled open the storeroom door and gaped at the sight.

An ornate and brightly colored coach pulled by two matching **dappled** gray horses was nearing the storeroom. A driver sat on the high front seat of the carriage, dressed in a close-fitting red jacket with shiny metal buttons and a black flattened cap, which was set sideways on his head. A red and yellow coat-of-arms on his sleeve indicated that he was in the service of nobility. The driver pulled the reins close to his chest. The horses stopped, dipping their heads and stepping in place, a sign that they had not tired on the journey to Gallant's home. The driver tied the reins to an iron hand rail, then climbed down from his seat to open the carriage door. At once, Sir Francis stepped out.

"Gallant," he said, "Collect your things and join me. This coach was sent to carry us to Thornbury Castle."

"Thornbury Castle?" Gallant could hardly believe what he heard. *A castle! This is even better than I could have hoped. I'll see knights and armor and sword-fighting. Finally!* Gallant ran back for his slate and the flask and bread his mother had sent with him. *So, Sir Francis must have told Mother and Father about the plan.* He returned to the coach and stood a moment, **gawking** at the shape and design. *Such colors!* Blue and yellow on the cab, red at the large spoked wooden wheels. *No farmer would ever have such a **gaudy** wagon. It must belong to the noble who rules over the castle. Who else would have the money for such a thing?* He approached the door of the coach and eagerly reached for the handrail to pull himself up onto the foot-rest.

Sir Francis stopped him. "Gallant, today we have a rare opportunity. You must be on your best behavior. We are going to take our class to the castle, where we shall meet young Lady

Grace, the niece of Edward Stafford, 3rd Duke of Buckingham. She will be accompanied by her tutor, Lady Clare. It is time you learned proper habits around women of importance."

Gallant's shoulders dropped, though he tried hard to hide his disappointment. *I'd rather be touring the castle than meeting with a girl.* There was no way to avoid the trip, so Gallant resigned himself to spending the day enduring a lesson on **etiquette.** He knew Sir Francis had already **devised** a plan for the occasion. "Yes, sir," he said glumly.

"You shall watch every move I make, and listen to my every word," Sir Francis continued. "When the opportunity arises, you will imitate what I have done. In this way, you will learn about anticipating a young woman's need and giving her every comfort within your reach."

Gallant nodded solemnly.

"And Gallant, do not underestimate these women. Women of the castle are highly educated, trained to assume the management of the royal businesses in the absence of the Duke or Earl. They handle finances, inspect the livestock and produce,—even discipline the servants, when necessary. They are not to be trifled with!"

Gallant wasn't sure what to expect. He remembered his lesson in the garden. *It's best if I don't talk much. I'll just watch and learn all I can.*

"All right," said Sir Francis, "Let us be on our way." Sir Francis waited while Gallant climbed aboard the coach and then he followed. The driver swung the half-door shut, securing the latch on the outside of the door. Then he climbed aboard and took up the reins.

The coach cabin was large enough to accommodate four adults, two facing forward and two facing to the rear, their knees meeting in the center. Gallant sat on the rear bench, facing forward, with Sir Francis across from him.

"Our lesson starts now," Sir Francis announced as he reached into the corner of the coach and pulled out a long scroll tied with a leather string. He handed it to Gallant, who untied the string and unrolled the scroll. *A map!* Just last week, Sir Francis had taught Gallant how to read a map, but as yet they had not used one to travel. Sir Francis leaned over and pointed to a small box on the map. "That is where we are headed," he said. "Thornbury Castle." He then pointed to another location on the map. "And that is where we are now. You must get us to the castle, Gallant. Call your instructions out to our driver. He awaits your orders."

Sir Francis leaned back in his seat, tipped his hat down over his eyes and settled in for a nap. Gallant forgot all about his disappointment. *This is a real test! Will I remember what Sir Francis taught me last week? All those symbols on the map! Do I know what they mean and which way north is and how distances are represented?* The horses snorted and pawed at the ground, impatient to get started. Gallant started to sweat.

"We are here," he spoke to himself, pointing to the spot Sir Francis had indicated. He scanned the area circling that section. He found Bristol on the map and ran his finger all the way to Thornbury. "We need to ride through town if we want to be headed in the right direction."

Gallant called out to the rider: "Follow the worn path past the large oak tree, then turn left until you reach the center of town."

The carriage started to move. Gallant knew the early stage of the journey from going to town with his family, but he had to rely on the map after they passed the town square. The ride to town gave him a few minutes to study the map and try to recall everything he had been taught.

Gallant used his thumb and placed it in the area on the map between his home and the town square. He knew this distance was about sixteen furlongs. He measured how many thumb-widths stretched between his home and Thornbury Castle. "Just beyond five thumb widths. Hmm, that means we'll be traveling more than eighty furlongs," he said aloud to himself. "A two-hour journey to the castle if the driver keeps the horses' pace at a fast walk."

The horses whinnied, eager to trot, but Gallant was focused intently on the map. He barely noticed the bumpy ride or the lurching of the carriage as it passed over the uneven ground. "Large **groves** of trees are represented by groups of arrows pointing upward," Gallant mumbled to himself. "Rivers are squiggly lines and bridges are small boxes over a river. Roads are fairly straight paths, represented by two parallel lines, as if they were made by the wheels of a coach."

Gallant glanced out the window of the carriage. They were still a short distance from town, but they were getting closer. He looked up at the sky and saw the sun angled to one side. *The sun rises in the east and since it is on the right side of the coach, this means we are headed north.* He looked back at the map. Maps were usually drawn with the north at the top of the map. Since the castle was closer to the top of the map than their house, they needed to go north to get there.

The line from his house to the castle was not straight. They had to cross a bridge and pass through two other small villages before they would arrive at the castle. Gallant leaned out the carriage window to call out to the driver: "Once you reach the town, follow the main road north out of the village. You should cross a bridge and come to a fork in the road. Take the fork to the right and stay on the path until you come to the next town." In the towns, the roads were more carefully maintained. Some were even paved with flat stones, which made the travel quicker and less bumpy.

The rider snapped the reins and the horses quickened their pace. Sir Francis woke from his nap and looked out the window at the passing countryside. Every now and then, the coach would pass a villager walking on the dusty road and Sir Francis would wave and call, "Greetings, friend." He always received a cheerful response.

Sir Francis closed his eyes and leaned his head back again. They rode in silence for three quarters of an hour, passing through the second town without incident. Gallant debated with himself whether he should wake his teacher now that the map was getting more difficult to discern. Several roads **merged** into the next town and then departed the town at different angles. As the coach approached the town, Gallant looked out the window anxiously for any landmarks that would help him determine which road to take. The map showed a ridge running roughly northeast to southwest, to the east of Thornbury Castle. Gallant could see a ridge in the distance. They needed to stay to the west of the ridge, but there were two roads west of the hill, one going north and one south. Gallant had to be sure he picked the right one. *It's the second road we must take.* Unfortunately, while he was studying the map, he missed the first road.

Sir Francis **stirred,** peered out the window and asked: "Does the road we must follow have a large boulder near it?"

Gallant looked quickly at the map. A dot was next to the second road, the one they needed to take. *That must represent the large rock.* Gallant leaned out the window and saw a boulder up ahead.

"This road, Driver! Take this road!" Gallant shouted.

The coach **lurched** sideways as the driver turned just a minute before they would have missed the road. *So, Sir Francis has been watching me all along.* Gallant exhaled loudly, grateful his teacher was observing him, even as he rested.

Sir Francis adjusted his hat and sat up in his seat. Judging by the time they had been on the road, Gallant knew they were nearing their destination. After passing a stretch of undisturbed wilderness, they came upon a herd of cattle grazing in the fields on both sides of the dirt road. *Wow! There must be two hundred head of cattle!* Twice, the driver slowed and whistled for a cow to move off the road.

"The hair on their hide hangs nearly to the ground. I've never seen the like!" Gallant said exuberantly.

"These cattle all belong to the Duke," Sir Francis explained. "They are a breed called Longhorn, brought from the highlands and raised mainly to pull the plows and to provide milk and cheese; but His Grace has been known to hold banquets that are rich with cattle meats." Their shaggy white hides set them apart from the short-haired red-hide cows Gallant was accustomed to seeing around Bristol.

The coach passed a grove of mature trees and came to a large open meadow dotted with bunches of a flowering yellow plant. Sir Francis pointed out the window. "The cow-herders move the cattle after the animals have grazed all the available grass. That yellow plant, called cowslip, often grows in the manure the cows leave behind."

Gallant mused, "Such a pretty little flower growing in the middle of a smelly pile!"

"Indeed." Sir Francis stared out over the field. "Beauty can sometimes be found in the most unlikely places, if one takes care to watch for it."

Just about that time, Sir Francis nudged Gallant and nodded his head toward the coach window. "Thornbury Castle." In the distance stood an enormous gray stone block castle surrounded by an extensive gray rubble rock wall. A watchtower jutted up from the inner grounds, offering an unobstructed view in every direction.

"The soldier on duty in the tower saw us some time ago." Sir Francis noted. "A castle tower gives the guards a significant advantage over an army coming against them in battle."

Gallant began to roll up the map, relieved to be nearly done with this test, and eager to study the grand edifice before him. The coach neared the walls of the castle's outer court, passing a cemetery that held the earthly remains of former residents. Still they rode on, along the extensive wall until they reached the worn path of an entrance. The stone construction of the outer court wall formed an impenetrable barrier, with occasional openings similar to windows, at a height out of reach for any who might intend harm. Along the top of the wall, projections like teeth had been built in even distance from each other.

"In times of peace such as these, a Duke of Buckingham has no need of fortified battlements," Sir Francis explained. "This castle now serves as a grand residence and not a fortress; but in times of war, those teeth you see, called merlons, offered the protection of a stone wall for the bowmen to duck behind during battle. The spaces between them, called crenels, would have allowed the pouring of hot oil down on any who might think to scale the wall." Gallant shuddered at the thought; but then he was distracted again by the sheer magnitude of the castle grounds. Merlons and crenels also topped the castle building inside the outer court walls, a stylish and practical design that made the massive structure all the more imposing.

The coach arrived at the arched entrance, where the outer court wall joined the castle gatehouse on either side. Someone from within called out forcefully: "Open for the Duke's Coach!" Suddenly the creaking and moaning of wooden timbers and metal rails signaled that the process had begun for lifting the enormous iron-studded wooden door that safeguarded the castle grounds. The coach passed through the archway and slowed as a column of foot soldiers passed in front of them, marching in coordinated step around the perimeter of the inner court. The footfalls of the coach horses on the smooth cobblestone created a rhythmic, almost musical cadence as they made their way through the streets; and now the subdued background of many voices revealed a vibrant city inside the court walls.

Gallant was overcome with emotion at being on the castle grounds. Until now, he had only seen castles from a distance. "Why would anyone ever leave?" he asked excitedly.

The knight smiled at his enthusiasm. "In warring times, everything the king and his soldiers needed was within the castle territory—food, provisions, weaponry and all the specialized craftsman to repair his fortress and maintain his defenses." The coach passed a row of merchant tents, bustling with activity. "In these quieter times, the Duke of the manor is more concerned about the success of his businesses; and the happiness of the Duchess." Sir Francis winked at Gallant.

"Merchants and buyers meet to discuss the newest clothing styles adopted by the king and his nobles," he continued. "Bolts of fabric are brought from afar and lined up on tables under the tents, kept out of the sun so they won't fade before they entice a buyer."

As they rode past, women stroked the fabric and chatted with one another. An eager merchant held a shimmering **translucent** veil against the **hennin** of a middle-aged woman who was dressed in silk and surrounded by attendants. A little farther on, farmers stood near wagons, laden with crops; while buyers poked the fruit and bantered with the sellers. Animal pelts hung in neat rows from a wooden rack, just above a small boy who sat on a workbench as a leatherman measured his foot for a pair of custom shoes.

Gallant remembered that his new friend James had moved to Thornbury. His father was the Duke's carpenter. Gallant looked for him anxiously in the crowds. Just as they made a turn, Gallant spied a large sign with a mallet affixed to it hanging over the door of a shop. There sitting on a bench out front was James, playing some type of flute.

"James! James!" Gallant called as he hung out the coach window, "It's me! Gallant!"

James looked up and saw Gallant as the carriage passed by. "Gallant!" he yelled back. He jumped up and ran after the coach, waving wildly. James hopped onto the foot railing at the carriage door, clinging to the handrail while the carriage continued moving. He handed Gallant the instrument. "My fatha helped me ta carve it, Gallant. I wan ye shood haf it."

"Wow. Thanks, James!" James stepped off the carriage and waved until Gallant was out of sight. Gallant showed the gift to Sir Francis.

"It is a **recorder**; and a fine one at that." Sir Francis announced after examining it. "The envy of the town to be sure." Gallant treasured the recorder. *The first melody I will learn is the one Mother hums for us after church. What a surprise I will give her!*

Sir Francis suggested Gallant leave the gift in the carriage when they got to the castle. The boy readily agreed and turned his attention back to the scene around him. Dozens of people milled about, talking, laughing and toting baskets of food and provisions. Merchants called out their wares until the distinctive squeaks and creaks of the carriage caused the crowds to pause momentarily, craning to see who was arriving in the Duke's coach.

"Sir Francis, my friend!" A merchant cupped his hands around his mouth to call out. "Come back for your Brie cheese. It sells quickly!"

Sir Francis took off his hat and used it to wave to the merchant. "Soon, Otto! Save two for me!"

The coach turned a corner and stopped for a farmer who was rolling his wooden cart of vegetables across the street in front of the carriage. Without warning, an old woman appeared at the door of the carriage. She wore bright colorful clothing and chunky pieces of jewelry.

"Francis! I would read your palm for half-a-crown. Give me a sovereign and I will curse your enemies!" Her voice sounded like a taunt, as if she dared the knight to accept her offer.

Sir Francis responded with a blistering command: "Be gone, old woman, and amend your ways! Sorcery belongs to the devil." Gallant had never seen his instructor speak this harshly to anyone. The carriage began to move, even as Sir Francis continued to stare at the woman, left standing in the street. Her cackle echoed off the stone walls. Without breaking his gaze, he stated firmly: "Those who lead others into this poison are guilty of the greatest sin. May the Lord forgive her." All Gallant could think about was what Sir Francis would say to him if he learned about what he had done in secret. *He would speak harsh words to me as well, and I would deserve them.* Soon the woman was out of sight, and Sir Francis returned to his task as teacher, once again pleasant and calm. Gallant tried to focus on his current task.

The coach approached the castle building. "Do you see those narrow slits in the walls, the ones in the shape of a cross?" Sir Francis asked. Gallant nodded quickly. "They are called arrow loops. They have been strategically positioned and built into the walls as a defensive post for archers. Inside, the thick walls have been tapered back around those openings, to give the archers a wider angle of attack. Even though the castle isn't now used for **siege**, when it was built nearly two hundred years ago, it would not have been constructed without some basic defenses."

Sir Francis pointed high above the arrow loops. Gallant's eyes traced the stone upward. Past the merlons and crenels at the top of the castle, two evenly twisted red brick columns soared above the building roofs.

"Those ornate chimneys vent the smoke of numerous fireplaces, but also display the talent of the Duke's brick masons," Sir Francis added. Gallant had never seen such detailed work.

Sir Francis continued, pointed to the building roof. "Slabs of slate cover the roofs, a deliberate choice meant to frustrate any attempts to burn the buildings down with fiery arrows." Slate was a dark gray rock that easily split into flat sheets and could be neatly arranged and attached as shingles onto only the most impressive buildings of the day. "When completed," Sir Francis continued, "slate creates a waterproof surface that will last for a century or more."

Gallant tried to impress the images on his mind, eager to describe every detail to his family when he returned home. *There's so much to remember!* The coach arrived at a prominent structure of the complex, a tall stone building.

"This is where the Duke and Duchess of Buckingham live with their family," Sir Francis said, watching Gallant's look of awe with a smile. "This well fortified structure is called the stronghold."

As the boy handed his teacher the map, the knight added, "Well done, Gallant." He tied the map with the rawhide string and set the scroll in the corner of the coach just as the driver jumped off his seat and swung open the carriage door.

Sir Francis spoke **cryptically** to Gallant. "Now your real test begins."

Think About This

Before electronic devices were invented to give driving directions, travelers used paper maps to find out what roads to take. Can you find a paper map and study the way it uses compass directions (north, south, east, west) and the way it shows the number of miles between cities?

dappled (sounds like **dap**-ell-d): an adjective, spotted, mottled

gawking (sounds like **gawk**-ing): a verb, being obvious in staring

gaudy (sounds like **gaw**-dee): an adjective, having overly bold or ornate decoration

etiquette (sounds like **et**-i-ket): a noun, proper or formal manners

devised (sounds like dee-**vized**): a verb, to make a plan to do something

groves (sounds like **grove**-z): a noun, clusters of trees

merged (sounds like **murr**-jd): a verb, to join together

stirred (sounds like **sterr**-d): a verb, to awake

lurched (sounds like **lurcht**): a verb, to move sideways awkwardly

translucent (sounds like trans-**loo**-cent): an adjective, see-through, but not clear

hennin (sounds like **hen**-nen): a noun, a tall, butterfly-shaped hat worn by the women in the Middle Ages

recorder (sounds like ree-**cor**-der): a noun, a cylindrical instrument with holes along its length, played by blowing into one end and covering holes with the fingers to alter the sounds

siege (sounds like **seej**): a noun, a war

cryptically (sounds like **krip**-tick-lee) an adjective, mysteriously

If you have the Sir Gallant Castle Kit, go to your Workbook now and complete the next lesson, called Banner 9.

CHAPTER TEN

Deep Within a Castle

The coach was stopped a few paces from the main entrance to the Duke of Buckingham's residence. Soldiers stood at attention at either side of the doorway, each wearing a chain mail coif and dressed in a chain mail shirt. Their armor was partially covered by the tabard bearing the Duke's coat-of-arms, a yellow shield with a red arrowhead filling the center. They stood tall and motionless, grasping the midsection of a spear, which rested on the ground at their feet. Each bore a short dagger at his waist on one side and a long silver sword on the other side, which hung from his waist nearly to the ground.

The driver held the carriage door as Sir Francis and Gallant climbed out of the coach and stretched. Gallant studied everything around him. The sounds and smells were very different than what the boy was accustomed to from living on a farm. The hammering of a blacksmith echoed toward them from around the corner, just out of sight. Gallant imagined a swordsmith was shaping the metal for a new sword. He had learned that metal had to be heated, folded and pounded to strengthen the integrity of the steel. He was sure that the distinctive *hissssss* in between the clanking was the red-hot sword being dunked into a large drum of water to quickly cool the metal as part of the forging process.

Sir Francis straightened his shoulders, tugged at his coat to pull out the wrinkles and brushed lint off his sleeve. He looked over at Gallant, who took his cue from the knight and quickly tucked in his shirt and tightened his belt.

"Gather your things," the knight instructed.

Gallant pulled the strap of his flask over his head and shoulder and then picked up his slate board and the loaf of bread and followed Sir Francis. Just past the castle entrance, several dark tunics and a long yellow dress hung from a rope strung between two tall stakes in the ground. A breeze swayed them all gently. Sir Francis walked toward the clothes line. As they approached it, the fragrant aroma of **sage wafted** past them.

Just the other side of the hanging clothes, a girl, about Gallant's age, was pulling weeds from among the sage, dill, coriander, and clover plants. A young woman in a long blue gown sat on a stone bench near her. She had brown hair pulled back into a graceful braided gathering, with curls falling loosely around her face. Her skin was like porcelain, clear and smooth. The young girl was humming a tune to herself, but she stopped and stood up as soon as she caught sight of Sir Francis and Gallant. The lady in blue watched them approach, but neither the woman nor the girl spoke a word.

Sir Francis bowed low and gestured toward Gallant. "God save you both. It is a delight to see you again. Lady Grace and my Lady Clare, this is Gallant, a student of knighthood." Lady Grace looked at Gallant and nodded as Sir Francis continued, "Gallant, I present Lady Grace, niece of the 3rd Duke of Buckingham. And this is Lady Clare, her tutor and chaperone." Gallant bowed low, as Sir Francis had done, and he spoke a careful greeting: "God save you, Lady Grace; and you, Lady Clare. It is my pleasure to meet you."

Lady Grace curtsied and Lady Clare nodded from her place, still seated on the bench. The girl Grace smiled shyly and replied, "God save you both. My uncle, His Grace, was called away unexpectedly on the King's business. He bid me pass his greetings to you."

The young girl wore a canvas smock over a **lavender**-colored linen dress. Her leather slippers had been dyed to match the color of her dress. *Lavender leather? How silly! They function just as well without dye.* Lady Grace's auburn hair was long, pulled back and held in place with a clasp made of an animal bone. Gallant had never before seen such an **extravagantly** dressed child. *How could anyone take care of a garden dressed like that?* The smock caught the dirt from the garden and kept it off her dress, but Gallant couldn't imagine why anyone would have such fancy clothing if it had to be covered up. Even though he was surprised by what he saw, Gallant tried not to stare—Sir Francis had warned him it was rude to do so. Instead, Gallant stood still and watched Sir Francis closely.

"Will you join us in our studies?" Sir Francis asked Lady Grace. The young girl dipped her head in a gentle 'yes.' She wiped her hands on her smock, removed it and handed it to Lady Clare, who laid it on the stone bench.

She turned back to Sir Francis: "I bid you escort Lady Clare to the book room." Sir Francis stepped closer and extended his right arm to Lady Clare, just as she rose from the bench. She placed her left hand over his sleeve and the two began to walk, Sir Francis escorting her toward the entrance of the stronghold. As they walked, he glanced back at Gallant, tipping his head slightly toward Lady Grace.

The boy suddenly realized that Lady Grace was waiting for him to escort her in the same way Sir Francis was escorting Lady Clare. He transferred his slate and loaf to his left hand and then stepped nearer to her and extended his right arm. She placed her left hand on his sleeve and the two began to walk, following Sir Francis and Lady Clare into the building. As Lady Grace approached the steps, she gathered her skirt in front with her right hand and lifted it slightly to prevent her from tripping on the long gown.

Gallant looked ahead to observe Sir Francis' movements. He noticed that the knight moved slowly and treated Lady Clare as though she were a queen. *Don't walk so fast, Gallant! Slowly, slowly!* Gallant and Lady Grace followed the knight and the lady past the soldiers posted at the entrance. Both men saluted Lady Grace by extending the tip end of their spears forward, while the other end remained in position on the ground. After she passed, each returned his staff to its upright position.

Gallant and Lady Grace followed Sir Francis and Lady Clare through a long corridor of stone. Iron sconces along the walls bore candles, lighting the way through the windowless hall, past a large greeting room on the left. The double-wide archway allowed Gallant an extra minute to study the details as he passed.

Heavy drapes hung at the arched entrance, held back by tasseled ropes, and the inner walls of the room were lined with dark wood. Tapestries of flower gardens and prancing horses decorated the rough outer wall, and rugs covered most of the stone floor, woven in sizes larger than anything his mother could make at the loom. Along the wall, a finely crafted narrow wood table bore various sized bottles of drink and a neat row of brown-tinted glass goblets. *Glass from Venice!* Gallant had only seen such fine glass once before on the King's table during a tournament. Two broad couches covered with ornate floral fabric were positioned adjacent to the hearth. The fireplace was well stocked with flaming blocks of wood.

Lady Grace spoke. "The fire is kept burning all hours of the day and night for unexpected visitors. My aunt, the Duchess, is known for her hospitality." Gallant nodded, hesitant to speak any more than necessary.

The four continued along the hallway. A doorway on the right led to a kitchen, where the clanking and stirring of pots revealed a half-dozen servants preparing the next meal for the Duke's family. Behind them a large fireplace, rimmed with long slabs of white stone, snapped with fresh wood. *Something smells delicious. Apple currant, perhaps?*

Sir Francis stopped and spoke to Lady Grace. "Gallant brings a gift for the Duke and Duchess. Would you accept it on their behalf?"

Lady Grace nodded, and so Gallant held out his loaf of bread.

"Edmund?" She called as she turned to the kitchen. An elderly manservant promptly arrived and received the loaf, bowed to Lady Grace and returned to the kitchen.

The four proceeded down the hall to where it ended, near the back of the castle. Lady Clare waited at the door until Sir Francis stepped in front and opened it for her. The heavy wooden door creaked with a deep groan. Gallant marveled at the layers of thick timber used to construct it. The artistic scrolls of each massive iron hinge extended past the centerline of the door. *Once closed and latched, surely no enemy could pass!*

Lady Clare had already begun to travel up a narrow limestone spiral staircase, grasping the twisted bronze handrail for balance. Since there was only room for one person at a time, Sir Francis followed behind her. Gallant escorted Lady Grace to the base of the staircase and then waited as she took the steps first. He followed behind, careful not to crowd her.

The stairs led them to a small room with tall leaded glass windows and intricately carved furniture. The scent of leather and sweet pipe tobacco greeted them, a new aroma to Gallant, rich and pleasant. The fireplace was barren of fire or embers, an indication that the room had not been used in at least two days. *This must be the Duke of Buckingham's study. Lady Grace said he had been called away on business.* As he passed an oak writing desk, Gallant ran his fingers along the smoothly sanded *bas relief* floral pattern inlaid into the desktop edges. The scrolls and vines on the desk and chairs required the skill of a master carpenter. *I wonder if James' father made these.* They passed through the room and on to what appeared to be a sitting area. A table was positioned at one end of the room, in front of three benches. Lady Clare was standing by the front bench. When Lady Grace joined her, the two immediately sat down.

Gallant stopped just inside the doorway, mesmerized by what he saw. Two walls were entirely covered with shelving, from floor to ceiling. One held a variety of books, but it was the other one that captured Gallant's attention. He counted five shelves filled with helmets, having such shapes and styles as Gallant had never before seen. Adjacent to the helmets, a bronze-tinted suit of armor was displayed on an iron stand. He rushed over and studied it closely, sighing **wistfully** as he marveled at the ornate engraved scrolling on the armor. *Surely this is the Duke's own suit! If only I could lift the helmet visor or try on the gauntlet. What harm is there in that?*

Gallant turned his attention back to the shelf full of helmets, standing close enough to smell the oil. He had learned from the town blacksmith that a fine layer of oil kept metal pieces from rusting. He waited for an invitation to examine the knights' headgear, but Lady Grace and Lady Clare were discussing the topic for class, and Sir Francis was too preoccupied with the books to notice, walking slowly past the volumes and studying the covers as he went.

Sir Francis considers the books more valuable than the armor! Gallant took a moment to look at the bookshelf, trying not to be obvious about his preference for the helmets. He noticed the variety in the book sizes and the manner in which they were bound. Some had ornate leather bindings with iron clasps holding them closed. Some were wrapped in cloth and tied. Many were large, thick books with ragged-edged pages.

Sir Francis turned to Gallant with a child-like excitement. "Most of these volumes were copied from the original by monks, highly educated religious men who lived a life of service in the solitude of a monastery." Sir Francis paused at the bookshelf, directing his attention to Lady Grace. "My Lady, should we have enough time, I would eagerly share the magnificence of these books with Gallant."

Gallant rolled his eyes. *Not the books, Sir Francis! The helmets! I want to see the helmets!* Gallant was relieved when he realized no one had seen his impatience. He composed himself. *Focus, Gallant. You are not here to play.*

Lady Grace nodded her approval. "His Grace recently acquired *Dante's Inferno*, printed by Aldus Manutius in 1508. The illustrations are exquisite." Sir Francis seemed delighted.

"Gallant," he said with enthusiasm, "you shall not find a finer collection!"

Gallant mustered up all the sincerity he could. "I am honored to be here. No doubt many would wish to see it," he said respectfully. He tried to absorb everything around him, eager to learn much from his first trip to a castle; but his gaze kept returning to the helmets. He decided his favorite was the one with a face-plate that would be lowered and latched in place during battles or jousts. A thin slit across the front gave the knight limited vision and the grated mouth area allowed adequate ventilation. For a moment, Gallant imagined he was encased in a metal suit ready to defend Lady Grace against a marauding band of thieves. The conversation around him brought him back to the classroom.

"One of my favorite rooms," Sir Francis was saying to Lady Clare. "I am grateful for the opportunity to share my knowledge with you both in such surroundings." Sir Francis took his place at the head of the classroom and motioned for Gallant to take a seat on the middle bench. Gallant understood that Lady Grace merited the most prominent place and should not be crowded by a stranger.

As always, Sir Francis began class with the prayer. Lady Grace and Lady Clare bowed their heads as he spoke. "May the Good Lord bless our efforts and pour His Wisdom upon us as we seek to please Him by our studies."

All three replied, "Amen."

"Lady Clare, what would you have me discuss today? What topic was to be your next lesson?"

"Thank you, Sir Francis. You honor us with your knowledge. I meant to instruct on the wheel and its applications," she responded. Sir Francis picked up the slate board on the table and nodded thoughtfully.

"Well, that could include everything from carriage construction to the milling of grain. So let's begin."

Gallant had just decided he would run to that narrow stairwell if he were playing hide-and-seek with his little brother. *I could go up or down the stairs without being seen, depending on Timothy's approach*. He stared at the armor in the corner of the room. *If I lived here, I would play my games wearing a suit of armor just like that one. It would make hiding more difficult, but it would give Timothy an advantage in finding me.* He imagined he was being fitted for his own breastplate when suddenly he realized Sir Francis had asked him a question. He sat up straight and responded meekly: "I do beg your pardon, Sir Francis. Would you repeat the question?" He noticed that Lady Grace was suddenly occupied with straightening her **bodice** as she sat, as if she were unaware of Gallant's deficient answer. Lady Clare adjusted Lady Grace's hair clasp. He appreciated these thoughtful gestures, meant to minimize his humiliation.

Sir Francis understood that the surroundings were distracting Gallant, so he didn't scold the boy. Instead, the knight answered the question for

Gallant and continued with the lecture, to Gallant's relief. *Focus on the task, Gallant!* Sir Francis had introduced the functionality of the wheel.

"We will turn our attention to the usefulness of pulleys." Sir Francis drew a simple diagram of a well with a single pulley fixed on a frame above the well. He held the board up for his students to see. As he drew the rope from the crank, running over the pulley and into the well, Lady Clare sneezed. Immediately, Sir Francis stopped his presentation and pulled a white kerchief from inside his jacket. With a slight bow, he handed it to Lady Clare and then resumed his teaching. It was a flawless movement, Gallant observed, almost as though Sir Francis knew that she would sneeze and he placed a clean kerchief right where he could get to it quickly. *So this is how a gentleman anticipates a need.*

Sir Francis returned his attention to the slate board. "One pulley at the top of the well allows a person to direct their force downward, rather than trying to lift the water up. Using their own body weight in conjunction with gravity, they can more easily draw the water than if they tried to lift it from the well without a pulley." Sir Francis drew another pulley, connected to the first. "If you were to add a second pulley, the weight is distributed over the wheels and the effect is that the bucket feels lighter. This advantage comes at a cost, however. Lessen the weight by half, and rope must be pulled twice as far as the bucket is lifted." The teacher paused for his students to contribute to the session. "What other uses does a pulley serve?"

Gallant was eager to join the conversation. "Lifting an armor-clad knight onto his steed."

"Ah, yes, on occasion." Sir Francis nodded.

"Hoisting hay and other grains to the lofts of barns," Lady Grace added.

"Indeed," responded Sir Francis. "You see how useful such a device has become in our daily lives. Consider, Lady Grace, the door at the entrance of the castle grounds. The portcullis, that large iron grate, drops down over the opening by the use of pulleys. The portcullis acts as a counterweight, to assist the men who operate the wooden door. It is an efficient use of men and mechanics; a vital necessity, were you ever forced to prevent an enemy from gaining access to the castle."

Sir Francis glanced out the window. "Lady Grace, Lady Clare, would you care for a short break, perhaps a few moments in the warm sun?"

They both readily agreed. As he stepped forward to Lady Clare, he glanced quickly at Gallant and tipped his head up in a slight movement, indicating Gallant should follow his lead. The boy immediately rose to his feet, just as Lady Clare took hold of Sir Francis' extended hand and stood. *That wasn't necessary*, Gallant observed critically. *Lady Clare is certainly capable of standing on her own.* But he remembered the knight's words: "Watch every move I make..." Gallant wrinkled his brow. *These small actions must be part of a knight's courteous behavior—even if they aren't really necessary.* He reached for Lady Grace's hand and helped her to stand.

Sir Francis moved to the door and held it open for Lady Clare to pass through. As she released his hand he bowed to her. Gallant did the same with Lady Grace. *Clearly, ladies expect these courtesies. They must have been taught this is how a gentleman behaves in their presence.*

After both walked out of their view, Gallant approached Sir Francis and stood near him in the doorway. **Exasperated**, he whispered to his teacher: "How can I possibly remember all the things I must do?"

Sir Francis laughed and patted Gallant on the shoulder. "Once you begin to forget yourself and think only of the needs of others, these courtesies come quite naturally."

"Wha-what does that mean? Forget myself? I don't understand." Gallant was beginning to think this part of knighthood was a puzzle he might never solve.

"Let's look at it a different way," Sir Francis suggested. "Are you thirsty?" Neither of the travelers had taken water from their flasks since they left the farm. Now that he thought about it, he was thirsty. Gallant nodded.

"So am I," Sir Francis said, "and yet a knight would not take a drink until he first offered his flask to any lady in his company." Sir Francis watched Gallant closely, to see if he understood.

"But—but—she lives in a castle and has servants to fetch water for her." Gallant shook his head. *That just doesn't make sense*. "She ought to offer fresh, cold water to us," he argued.

"But that is not what a gentleman would expect. Or allow."

There was a sudden breakthrough in Gallant's thinking. "And knights are, first and foremost, gentlemen," he announced with newfound clarity. Sir Francis looked past Gallant to the shelving.

"I know you are eager to study the armor. Go while we have a short break." Gallant rushed to the shelf. He still had not been given permission to touch the helmets, so he merely looked at each one from every angle. About a quarter of an hour passed before Lady Grace and Lady Clare returned. Sir Francis held the door open wide and both the knight and the boy bowed to them as they neared. Lady Grace carried a tray of green apple tarts seasoned with saffron spice. Fresh from the oven, the tarts filled the room with a delicious aroma.

The four sat at the table, Sir Francis said a brief prayer, and together they enjoyed the unexpected treat. Gallant opened his flask of water and offered it first to Lady Grace. After her sip, she complimented Gallant on the purity of the water: "As fresh as a newfound spring!" Gallant offered the flask next to Lady Clare. She smiled and held her hand up, a kind way of declining.

Gallant glanced up at Sir Francis. *Well done*, the teacher conveyed silently with his wink and nod.

Within a few minutes they returned to their studies. Gallant settled in and learned how to focus on his task, despite the fascinating variety of items all around him. Before he knew it, class was over, and he was escorting Lady Grace as they followed Sir Francis and Lady Clare back to the carriage. When they exited the stronghold, Lady Clare stopped and stepped aside, speaking quietly with Sir Francis as Gallant and the young girl approached.

As the two young students passed the soldiers, Gallant noticed the clothing on the line had been removed. A row of colorful wildflowers grew in a straight line on the ground, directly under the rope. He hadn't noticed them before. Gallant stared a minute, considering whether they had been planted there. Lady Grace noticed his gaze.

"The flowers grow from the seeds dropped by the birds that perch on the rope. I only know because I saw it happen once. I've asked the maids not to step on them."

Gallant recalled the words of Sir Francis. He spoke thoughtfully. "Beauty can sometimes be found in the most unlikely places, if one takes care to watch for it." Lady Grace seemed pleasantly surprised by his comment. She smiled, nodding her agreement, just as they arrived at the waiting coach.

"I am certain my uncle would have enjoyed your company." Lady Grace said to Sir Francis.

"And I, his." Sir Francis answered. "Yet even in his absence, it was my honor to teach his lovely niece. Please pass our gratitude to His Grace for such kind hospitality and for the exquisite transportation." He bowed deeply, then looked to Lady Clare. "My delight to see you again, my lady." She curtsied in response.

The young girl nodded. "Sir Francis, perhaps on your return trip, you could reserve time to examine the books."

The knight smiled broadly, glancing over at Lady Clare. "I look forward to the day."

Gallant bowed to Lady Grace and then to Lady Clare in imitation of his tutor. "Thank you, Lady Grace, for the delicious meal," he said sincerely.

"Thank you for the loaf, Master Gallant. We will enjoy it with supper," she replied.

"I am, um, we are, that is—my family is honored that our gift will be on your table today." Gallant responded. He flushed with embarrassment at his stumbling of words; but once again, those present were so polite that it was as if they hadn't even noticed.

Lady Grace seemed to appreciate Gallant's effort. She smiled at him. "Safe travels. God be with you."

Sir Francis and Gallant climbed into the carriage for the ride back home, but the coach did not move until Lady Grace and Lady Clare had returned to the castle. Once they were out of view, the driver snapped the reins, and the horses began the journey back through the castle grounds. Sir Francis continued his instruction. "What makes Lady Grace a woman of importance?" he asked Gallant.

Gallant thought a moment before responding. "She comes from a wealthy family. Her uncle owns the castle and the land around it. He's a very important man in the community."

Sir Francis was not satisfied with the answer. "And yet, your mother has none of those things, and she is a woman of importance, is she not?"

"Of course she is!" he **retorted**, protesting even the suggestion that she was anything less. "She takes care of my father and my brother and sister and me. She is very important."

Sir Francis nodded and then asked: "Your little sister cannot yet care for anyone, nor is she the niece of the Duke of Buckingham, and yet, she is also important. Yes?"

Gallant was starting to understand that all women, old and young, were important. He needed to find what made them so, if he ever hoped to learn the lesson that Sir Francis was trying to teach him. He considered all the things that Lady Grace had in common with Lady Clare, and his mother, his sister, and his Aunt Miriam.

Sir Francis prodded him: "Remember the old woman you met in the woods? Did she have any children who would have thought her important?"

Gallant shrugged. "I don't know. I didn't know anything about her."

Sir Francis continued, "Well, did she have a mother?"

Gallant laughed. "Yes! Everyone has a mother! How else would they be born?" And suddenly, he realized what Sir Francis was trying to teach him. He chose his words carefully and spoke slowly. "All women are loved, and that makes them important to someone."

Sir Francis turned to the boy and added: "And that, Master Gallant, makes them important to us. Do you understand?" When Gallant nodded, his teacher continued the lesson. "Now, what have you learned today?"

Gallant was ready with his response. "All women are women of importance."

"That's it!" Sir Francis clapped his hands together and grinned.

I got it. Gallant smiled to himself. A moment passed as Gallant's smile slowly disappeared into a look of confusion. "Wait," he said. "What about the old woman who wanted to tell your fortune? Is she a woman of importance too?"

Sir Francis grew somber. "Yes, Gallant, she is. But alas, she has forgotten what it is that made her so. Whenever I encounter her, I speak only truth, hoping to shake her out of her delusion. But no matter how she responds, I will not pretend that her life of sorcery and magic is acceptable. It is not loving or respectful to affirm someone in their sinful behavior." Sir Francis leaned forward, grasped Gallant's shoulder and met his gaze. "Know this: love demands truth."

Sir Francis leaned back and tipped his hat over his eyes for the trip home.

Gallant didn't realize how exhausted he was until he had been sitting for a few minutes, enjoying his success with the lesson. He picked up his new recorder and blew into it, creating a few disorganized sounds. He set it in his lap to rest his eyes for a moment, and without warning, an angry thought entered his mind. *You were brought to a castle and didn't learn one thing about being a knight. Sir Francis mocks you! You're a fool to think he is teaching you anything worthwhile.*

Gallant opened his eyes and shook his head. The knight sat across from him, resting peacefully. *No, Sir Francis is an honorable knight. He knows best . . . doesn't he?* Gallant was exhausted by the travel and the day of learning, and he had no energy left to consider whether or not he was being treated fairly. Before the carriage reached the cow fields, Gallant was sound asleep. The young boy didn't realize that a small seed of **discontent** had been planted.

1. Gallant learned how he should act around the niece of the 3rd Duke of Buckingham. But shouldn't these courtesies also apply to women who are *not* part of a royal family?

2. Lady Grace had been taught the fineries
   of hospitality. This means that she took
   actions that made the visitors feel very
   welcome in her home. Do you think these
   actions apply to all visitors or just family
   and friends?

coif (sounds like **coyf**): a noun, a hat, similar
   to a hood

sage (sounds like **say-j**): a noun, an herb used in
   cooking

wafted (sounds like **wahf**-ted): a verb, to blow past,
   carried by the wind

lavender (sounds like **lav**-n-der): a noun, a flower
   with a pleasant fragrance, also a shade of the
   color purple

extravagantly (sounds like eggs-**trav**-a-gant-lee): an
   adverb, in a very fancy way

currant (sounds like **ker**-rent): a noun, a small
   round fruit used in baking

bas relief (sounds like baaa-ree-**leaf**): a noun, type
   of art wherein objects project slightly from a
   surface

wistfully (sounds like **wisst**-full-lee): an adverb, with yearning or longing for something

bodice (sounds like **bod**-iss): a noun, the part of a dress from the waist to the neck

courtesy (sounds like **kur**-tess-see): a noun, a polite action meant to show respect or bring comfort to another (plural: courtesies)

exasperated (sounds like ex-**asp**-ur-ated): a verb, irritated and annoyed

retorted (sounds like ree-**tort**-id): a verb, to respond to something with force and emphasis

discontent (sounds like diss-kahn-**tent**): an adjective, a feeling of dissatisfaction

If you have the Sir Gallant Castle Kit, go to your Workbook now and complete the next lesson, called Banner 10.

CHAPTER ELEVEN

Art of the Letter

Gallant had always been curiously drawn to the chanting of the choir at Mass; and he loved his mother's joyful singing around the house and in the garden, but it wasn't until he received the recorder from James that he found he had a genuine talent for music. He quickly mastered his mother's favorite tune and delighted her with his **rendition** as she prepared supper. He blew the last note out in a long, dramatic ending, bowing as he finished. His mother hugged him warmly. "Such a thoughtful gift to play my favorite melody, Gallant! How lovely of you."

Gallant practiced the music scale on his recorder, beginning with the lowest note he could play and ending with the highest. As he memorized the position of his fingers for each note, he expanded his **repertoire**. He taught himself a faster-paced melody he had heard in town, tapping his foot to keep a steady beat. As he played, Margaret danced around the trestle table, swinging her blue dress until it looked like the top of an acorn. When he finished his performance, Margaret clapped her hands, begging for more music. Timothy pulled his fingers out of his ears, where he had firmly lodged them as soon as Gallant began to play. His angry pout was a dramatic show of displeasure for the shrill noise of the recorder.

"Hmmm. You might like it better if you were playing." Gallant handed the recorder to Timothy, who promptly blew a squeak that sounded something like the yelp of a puppy. Gallant stood behind him and helped him to hold the recorder, with Gallant arranging his own fingers for different notes as Timothy inhaled and exhaled into it. The result was one small portion of a lullaby their mother often sang to them at bedtime, although it came out a bit choppy. Timothy beamed with satisfaction. Gallant had won him over.

I wonder if I will ever return to Thornbury to show James what I have learned. Gallant had made even more progress after Sir Francis encouraged him to play the instrument whenever he had a few minutes between assignments or chores.

"Never waste a moment, Gallant," Sir Francis had said. "Time does not return once it is spent."

Gallant began to carry his recorder tucked in his belt as he completed his chores around the farm, tooting on it as he walked to the well; or when he rested after raking out the stable. He brought it to class along with his slate and chalk, picking it up anytime there was a break in his lesson. Sometimes he even had a few minutes before class, and he eagerly used the time to practice.

But not today. Today he was not interested in playing his recorder.

When Gallant arrived for his lesson, he found a beautiful **quill** pen and a bottle of ink at his desk. *The last time I saw a quill pen was when I accompanied Father to church, to register the birth and baptism of Timothy.* On that day, Gallant had watched as the priest dipped a feather into a bottle of ink and began to write. The feather was hollow, like a thin tube, and the ink collected in the tube when the priest dipped it into the inkwell. As the priest wrote, the ink drained from the feather and remained on the paper in handsome strokes. Gallant was so excited to see a quill pen up close that he almost picked it up. But the quill did not belong to him, and he had no right to touch it unless the owner gave him permission.

When Sir Francis entered the storeroom, Gallant stood up quickly and bowed. "Good morning Sir Francis," he said cheerfully.

"Good morning to you, Gallant," he responded. "May the Good Lord bless our efforts and pour His Wisdom upon us as we seek to please Him by our studies. I see you have found your new quill. You may examine it."

My new quill? Really? Gallant sat down and picked up the quill pen gently. The feather must have been from a wild turkey. It was cream in color, with long strands jutting outward for the most part and short soft strands near the writing tip. Delicate at one end, stiff and pointed at the other. Gallant was eager to start writing with it.

By now, Sir Francis had hung his hat and was standing at his place in the front of the classroom. "Do you know how to use a quill pen, Gallant?"

"Not exactly," he responded. "I watched someone once, though." Gallant hoped when he used the quill, it would work for him the same way it worked for the priest. Gallant already knew how to print his letters, but he had only learned **script** letters a few classes ago and he was still practicing them. Besides, until now he had only written with chalk on his slate board.

Sir Francis brought a sheet of homemade paper to Gallant. Not many people needed paper where Gallant lived because most people were farmers or bakers or shopkeepers. But Sir Francis was a learned man and many of the townspeople would come to him to write letters for them or to prepare bills of sale for land or **livestock**. Sir Francis had brought Gallant paper from his own supply. It had a small "F" stamped into the paper in the upper right corner.

"I can't tell you how to write with a quill, Gallant," Sir Francis began. "There is no talking about something that must be practiced if it is to be learned." Sir Francis sat next to Gallant at his desk and picked up the quill pen. He dipped it into the bottle of ink before him, tapped off an excess drip, and began to write. As the boy watched in amazement, Sir Francis wrote Gallant's name using handsome, neat strokes. Gallant observed every movement as the teacher dipped the pen again and wrote more words. Gallant saw how far down into the bottle the quill was dipped and how many seconds Sir Francis held it in the ink. He watched as Sir Francis tapped the point lightly, so not a drop of the ink would be wasted, and he watched as the ink drained from the quill as Sir Francis wrote. When the ink was nearly gone, but before it actually ran out, Sir Francis dipped it again. Gallant was eager to try.

Sir Francis set the quill pen down in front of Gallant and motioned for him to pick it up. Gallant used his left hand to position the quill in his right hand. He turned the quill slightly, so the full bloom of the feather **cascaded** over his right hand. Now he was holding the quill like Sir Francis had demonstrated. He dipped the pen and set the point of the quill on his paper. Immediately, a large blob of ink formed on the paper. Gallant quickly lifted the pen off the paper, but the ink continued to drip from the quill and left several drops of ink wherever Gallant moved his hand.

"Gallant," said Sir Francis calmly, "the ink doesn't stop flowing just because you stop moving the pen." Sir Francis tipped Gallant's hand sideways, so the quill was **horizontal**, and the dripping stopped. Embarrassed, Gallant nodded and tried again. He dipped the pen and quickly began to write. But this time, he pressed too hard and the tip of the quill tore the paper. Gallant looked at Sir Francis, frustrated and disappointed in himself.

Sir Francis laughed merrily. "Apply a little less pressure, Gallant. Pretend you are stroking the nose of a newborn lamb." Gallant dipped the quill and tried again, softly. He wrote his name in script. His words were not nearly as neat as Sir Francis' had been, but the ink was steady and lasted all the way through his name. This time the paper didn't tear. Gallant dipped the pen again. In script, he wrote: "Sir Francis" and then "Mother and Father, Margaret and Timothy." As Gallant continued to write, his use of the quill improved. When he stopped writing to have a look at his work, he held the pen horizontally, as Sir Francis had shown him.

Sir Francis nodded and walked to his lectern at the front of the classroom. "To whom shall we write, Gallant?" Sir Francis asked in a way that made Gallant think he already knew the answer.

"You would know better than I, sir," Gallant responded respectfully.

The teacher walked to a window of the storeroom and looked out over the fields. "Have you a relative in a distant town?" he asked.

Gallant's face brightened. "Uncle Gregor and Aunt Miriam own a flour mill that is a two-day journey by horse, Sir Francis. We last visited them three years ago."

Sir Francis turned to Gallant. "You will write to your Aunt Miriam. What will you say?"

Gallant blurted out the first thing that entered his mind. "Dear Aunt Miriam, how are you? I am fine."

Sir Francis exhaled loudly. "Bah!" He paced back and forth in the front of the classroom. "That would not be worth the ink used to write it," he said **brusquely**.

Gallant looked down at the quill and thought carefully before he spoke again. "They are my godparents, Sir Francis. Last time I saw them, my Uncle Gregor helped me to memorize the *Pater Noster*. I have not forgotten it."

"Much better. Now tell me something about your aunt that warms your heart."

Gallant paused and then his eyes lit up. "Mother told her how much I love cranberry rolls. She had some of them baking when we arrived, and when we came in the door, the whole house was filled with the smell of fresh baked rolls."

Gallant could see Sir Francis was pleased. "Do they have children?"

"Yes, yes! Two...my cousins! We had so much fun together." Gallant was eager to begin.

Sir Francis handed Gallant a new sheet of paper. "So, let's turn that into a letter," instructed Sir Francis. "What about that prayer? Do you ever say it? And didn't you just purchase a cranberry roll from the bakery the other day? And what made playing with your cousins so fun?"

Gallant nodded eagerly.

Sir Francis had one more instruction. He had a very serious look on his face as he spoke it. "Gallant," he started, "things you write last far longer than things you say. Be certain you write only those words you want another person to remember about you. Do you understand?"

Gallant raised his eyebrows and nodded slowly.

"Well, then," Sir Francis continued, "put your thoughts to verse, Gallant. And be sure to show your concern for them by inquiring about their well-being."

Again, Gallant picked up his quill, and this is what he wrote:

My Dear Aunt Miriam,
Greetings from Bristol!
I miss playing with my cousins.
I still remember climbing your
quince tree with Richard! That
same day, we taught Anne
how to fish! We had such
fun. Is everyone well? I just
learned how to use a quill pen
today. Sir Francis is teaching me
to be a knight. One day, he rewarded
me with a cranberry roll after I
completed an errand for him.
It was good, but it would have
been all the better coming from
your stone oven. I still remember
the prayer Uncle Gregor taught me.
Please thank him for me. It is
the perfect prayer for a knight, and
I intend to say it every day.
If the Lord will it, one day
I shall arrive at your door, dressed
in a suit of armor and riding
my trusty steed. Until then,
God save you all.
    Respectfully yours,
        Gallant

When Gallant finished, he placed the quill down and read the letter aloud. Sir Francis looked over Gallant's shoulder. When Gallant finished, Sir Francis handed him a new sheet of paper. "It's a fine letter, Gallant, but you've dripped ink—and your writing could be neater. Try again."

Gallant took a deep breath and set the letter aside as he positioned the new paper in front of him.

"This time," said Sir Francis, "begin your letter with some artwork. Let's decide on a design for the letter 'M,' the first letter in the first word of your note."

Gallant was confused. "How do we turn a letter into artwork?"

Sir Francis sat down beside him. Using the first page Gallant had practiced on, he wrote a letter "F" and then drew vines and leaves all around it. He drew a square around the outside of the letter and drew a bird perched on the top bar of the "F." When he was done, it was like a picture. Then Sir Francis wrote the rest of his name after the "F" so the "F" was very large and the other letters were smaller.

Gallant picked up his quill and thought a moment. He loved to draw dragons, and he had become fairly **proficient** at making them look scary, but he didn't want to scare Aunt Miriam. He kept thinking. "I shall draw a coat-of-arms," he said proudly. Gallant drew the letter "M" inside a shield and added scrolls and flags, designs he had seen on banners at the town fair. Then he copied his words to Aunt Miriam onto the new paper. When he was finished, Sir Francis instructed him to allow the ink to dry before he rolled the paper and tied it with a string. Sir Francis promised to deliver the letter to a friend who had business in Aunt Miriam's town the following month. She would have the letter by the end of summer.

Sir Francis taught Gallant how to swish the tip of the quill pen in water until the ink was washed out, so it would be clean and ready for the next writing assignment. When Sir Francis signaled that class was dismissed, Gallant stood and bowed. Sir Francis collected his hat from the hook on the wall, and gathered his books into his satchel. As he exited the storeroom, Gallant followed behind him, cocking his head to the side as he watched Sir Francis mount his horse and gather the reins. *Something's different about Sir Francis, but I don't know what it is.* He studied his teacher, holding up his hand to shield his eyes from the late morning sun.

"I shall see you the day after tomorrow, Gallant," the knight said as his horse trotted away.

As he watched Sir Francis ride into the woods, it suddenly occurred to Gallant. *Why, his feather is missing from his hat!* The quill pen Gallant had been using was made from the feather that had previously been in Sir Francis' hat. *Father said it is a sign of great status to wear a large bird feather in one's hat.*

Sir Francis had given Gallant the quill, without a word about his sacrifice in giving such a fine gift to the young boy. *Generosity is one of the qualities of a knight.*

"Someday, I too shall give away things of great value and meaning, and I shall be a true knight," said Gallant. He bowed again out of respect for Sir Francis, even though Sir Francis was already too far away to see it.

Think About This

1. How is writing a letter different from talking to someone in person or by telephone? How is it different than sending an e-mail or a text message?

2. What if you were to write a letter to a friend or relative? What kinds of information would you include? What questions would you ask?

Word Helper

rendition (sounds like rhen-**dish**-un): a noun, a particular version or interpretation

repertoire (sounds like **rep**-er-twahr): a noun, a list of songs, plays or other parts a singer or actor is able to perform

quill (sounds like kwill): a noun, the hollow and hard part of a feather, where it attaches to a bird

script (sounds like **skript**): a noun, fancy writing where all letters in a word are joined together

livestock (sounds like **live**-stock): a noun, a general name for farm animals

cascaded (sounds like cass-**ka**-did): a verb, to flow down artfully or in a beautiful manner

horizontal (sounds like hoar-i-**zon**-tell): a noun, to line up with the horizon, to go straight across from left to right, level with the ground

brusquely (sounds like **brus**-klee): an adverb, to do something abruptly, discourteously

Pater Noster (sounds like **pah**-ter-**noss**-ter): a noun, the Latin name for the Lord's Prayer, translated "Our Father"

proficient (sounds like pro-**fish**-ent): an adjective, to do something skillfully

If you have the Sir Gallant Castle Kit, go to your Workbook now and complete the next lesson, called Banner 11.

CHAPTER TWELVE

Animal Allies

Williams and Catherine had **bartered** for a young colt just a few years after they were married. They called the horse "Noctu" (which means night) because they brought him home on Midwinter Day, the day with the longest and darkest night. It was a perfect name. Just after they washed him, his dark coat shone black with a deep midnight-blue tint. Gallant was convinced Noctu must have known what a handsome horse he was. Whenever Gallant accompanied his father to town to visit the blacksmith, the **farrier** would offer to buy their horse, and William would laugh quietly and say again that he wasn't for sale. Noctu would toss his head in the air and snort as if to say, "I am no ordinary horse you know!" Gallant noticed people passing by would stop to admire their horse and comment about his shiny coat or his long mane and tail.

Gallant helped William care for the horse, which meant feeding him, brushing him, and hauling the manure out of the stable. As a reward for his effort, Gallant could ride Noctu in a big circle in the field. At first, William held on to a rope tied around the horse's neck. The lead rope didn't hurt the animal, but it let him know William was watching closely. Noctu always behaved. Little by little, William allowed Gallant more time on the horse and more control in riding him.

"You've got a way with him," William had once told Gallant as Noctu trotted past them both. "He listens to you, even seems eager to please you." By the time Gallant turned nine, he was already an accomplished rider; so much so that William had sent Gallant on errands to town, giving permission for the boy to ride at a gallop part of the way. Gallant enjoyed spending time with Noctu, often brushing him longer than necessary. It seemed to have a calming effect on them both.

One warm sunny morning, Gallant was making his way to the storehouse for class when he noticed Sir Francis had arrived early and was taking the saddle off of his horse. Usually Sir Francis just left the saddle on his horse and allowed it to **graze** while he taught Gallant. As the boy approached Sir Francis, he called out: "Excuse me, Sir Francis. Will we meet inside or outside today?"

Sir Francis waved Gallant over to him. "Outside, Gallant. May the Good Lord bless our efforts and pour His Wisdom upon us as we seek to please Him by our studies. Find the boar brush, will you?" Sir Francis signaled to a burlap sack on the ground. When Gallant opened it, he found several items he recognized as tools used to care for horses. He located the brush and reached out to hand it to Sir Francis, but the teacher was busy removing the blanket from his horse's back. He folded the blanket over the fence and then turned to Gallant.

"You've seen Donato, my steed, often enough. But you've never really met him, have you?" Sir Francis said with a wink.

Gallant squinted at Donato through the morning light. He was taller and stockier than Noctu, with a radiant chestnut-brown coat and neatly trimmed black mane. His legs were dark, as if he had waded through an ebony **lagoon.** *I'll be riding a knight's steed today! That's why this lesson is outside; with Sir Francis' horse, not Noctu.*

"Do you know how to brush a steed?" Sir Francis asked.

Gallant nodded. "If the same technique is used on a farm horse, then yes." Gallant understood what "steed" meant: this horse had carried a knight. Only horses that were muscular and **agile** could claim this honor, because their work was so different from that of a farm horse. Knights wore heavy armor, and the extra weight would tire ordinary horses. Knights also needed a mount that could quickly turn and spin, responding to the commands of the rider as he competed in the tournaments.

Sir Francis smiled at Gallant's response. "Indeed, we do brush a steed in the same way we brush a farm horse. You may begin. That's a good lad."

Gallant began to brush the steed's flanks, starting with the left side. As he reached up to the horse's back, he realized Donato was much taller than Noctu and had very **pronounced** muscles in his legs and back and neck.

The horse snorted and stomped his foot. "Don't brush so harshly that you redden his skin," Sir Francis corrected Gallant. He laughed and said, "Just because he's bigger than your farm horse doesn't mean his hide is thicker."

Gallant slowed his brushing and used less pressure, methodically working his way from one side of the horse to the other, careful not to miss any areas. Without needing to be told, he reached back into the bag on the ground for a softer brush to use on Donato's legs. Then he found a comb and untangled all the snarls in Donato's mane. The thorough grooming took a long time, especially for an animal this large and important.

Gallant was careful not to walk behind Donato without running his hand along the horse's flank. Letting the horse know where he was helped prevent an unexpected kick from the horse's hind legs. Horses were beautiful, regal animals, but Gallant knew they could be spooked easily, and a kick could be deadly. "Donato is so calm," he murmured, taking a step back and admiring the animal.

"Not only calm, but now he is once again neatly groomed," said Sir Francis, complimenting Gallant's work. "Do you know why we brush the steed's coat?"

Gallant always thought it was for the same reason people combed their hair: to keep it from getting matted or snarled. But when he conveyed the idea to Sir Francis, he learned something new.

"Lend me your shoe for a moment, Gallant." Sir Francis said. It was an odd request, but Gallant knew better than to question his instructor. He obediently removed his leather shoe and handed it to the knight, who bent to the ground and picked up a small pebble, no bigger than a ladybug. He dropped the pebble in Gallant's shoe and handed the shoe back. "Put it back on," he said. Gallant did as he was told. He felt the pebble under his toes. "Now," continued Sir Francis, "take a few steps."

The stone struck Gallant's foot every time he took a step, which caused him to walk slowly and set his foot down gently, limping when he put weight on the pebbled-shoe. After just a few steps, Gallant stopped and looked with pleading eyes at Sir Francis. "Enough, sir?" Gallant asked.

Sir Francis nodded. Relieved, Gallant quickly removed his shoe and shook the pebble out. Sir Francis patted the horse's neck as he spoke to Gallant. "In order to ride a horse comfortably and safely, we add a blanket and then a saddle.

The saddle must be tightened around the horse's belly snugly so it does not slip sideways and cause the rider to fall. If dirt or twigs, or even a small stone is left on the animal's coat and the saddle is tightened over it, the saddle will press the object against the skin and cause painful sores."

After experiencing the pebble in his shoe, this made perfect sense to Gallant. Sir Francis continued: "If we treat our animals well, they will enjoy the service they perform for us."

The knight reached into his saddle-pack and pulled out a large leather glove. He slipped it over his hand and his arm all the way to his elbow. "Stand clear," he ordered.

Gallant took a few steps back, bewildered at the strange command. Sir Francis turned and looked up toward the sky, where a large bird circled high above them. Sir Francis held up his arm, and the bird swooped downwards.

"Watch out, Sir Francis!" the boy shouted, dropping to the ground and covering his head with his arms. But neither Sir Francis nor his horse appeared alarmed. When Gallant glanced up, the bird was perched on Sir Francis' gloved hand, and Sir Francis was feeding it a small piece of dried meat.

Gallant slowly returned to his feet, feeling embarrassed. "I—I didn't know you had a falcon, Sir Francis."

Sir Francis held the bird lower so that Gallant could get a closer look. He had only seen falcons on one other occasion, when they were performing at the town fair. Gallant knew falcons could be trained to hunt wild game and bring their catch back to their owner, who was called a falconer. The falconer usually trained the falcon for many months before they went hunting together.

"What keeps my falcon returning to me, Gallant?" Sir Francis asked.

Gallant worked through the question in his mind. *Once the falcon is released from the glove, there are no strings to keep him from flying away forever. And when he catches his prey, why would he want to bring it back to the falconer instead of eating it himself?* Gallant was stumped. "I guess I don't know, sir."

"Animals know when they are treated well, and they know when they are treated badly," Sir Francis responded. "Throughout all our time together, I have never abused this falcon, nor caused him pain. Nor have I given him a reason to want to leave me. We have established a partnership, and it will not easily be broken." Sir Francis raised his arm quickly. The falcon flew away.

Gallant could see it circling far above them before it flew out of sight. Sir Francis stood quietly and waited. Within a few minutes, the falcon was back in view, with something clutched in its **talons**. As the falcon drew near, Gallant could see it was a wild turkey, a young one. The falcon released the turkey to Sir Francis before it perched on his glove again.

"Run quickly, and inform your mother I intend to stay for supper today," Sir Francis instructed Gallant. "Tell her I will bring her the turkey after it has been cleaned."

Gallant headed for home just as Sir Francis released the falcon and removed the glove. Until then, he had been so preoccupied with the falcon that he had forgotten Sir Francis had not allowed him to ride Donato. When he did remember, a flash of heat burned his face. *What a rotten trick, making you think you would ride a knight's horse, when all you get to do is the work of brushing him. Another lesson with no real knight training.* He mind was suddenly flooded with images of the work he had done for Sir Francis. *Running to market and settling accounts for him.* Gallant began to feel as though he had been cheated. He formed a list in his mind of the ways he had been insulted. He narrowed his eyes and gritted his teeth. *That's it. I will not be mocked any more. I'm done with these foolish lessons.*

When Sir Francis arrived at William and Catherine's home later that day with the turkey, Gallant stayed in the stable, restocking the straw bedding in Noctu's stall. Already it was unusual that his mother had to call him for supper, but when he came to the table, he refused to eat the turkey. After watching his son push the food around his plate for half the meal, William had enough.

"Gallant, you act as though you were a hedge-born rascal. Off to bed with you!"

With a scowl, Gallant left the table, kicked off his shoes and crawled into his bed, fully dressed. Catherine's face flushed with embarrassment. She and William had taught Gallant proper manners, and this **breach** of etiquette was unacceptable. Sir Francis broke the awkward silence. "I once knew an **impertinent** young lad whose brashness caused his parents great anguish," he said quietly.

William and Catherine exchanged a quick glance as Sir Francis nodded to indicate he was speaking of himself. "I can assure you that the efforts of a loving parent are never wasted," he added. "Be at peace."

William stood and retrieved a bottle of French wine he had been saving for a special occasion. He poured the deep **burgundy** liquid into three pewter goblets. The adults all held them up as William led the toast: "In thanksgiving for our many blessings; even the ones that, for a time, are hidden from our view."

"Here, here." Sir Francis chimed in, looking past Catherine to Gallant as he lay in his bed, wrapped tightly in his blanket, his back to their guest.

Think About This

1. Why do you think it is important to treat animals kindly?

2. What would you do if you saw someone being cruel to an animal? What if someone was being cruel to a person?

3. When a person is rude, do they harm the person they intended to insult or do they harm themselves?

bartered (sounds like **bar**-terd): a verb, to trade items or services of value

farrier (sounds like **fair**-ee-r): a noun, a person who makes horseshoes; in the Middle Ages, a farrier also treated ailments of the horse

graze (sounds like **grays**): a verb, to feed on the grasses and plants in a field or meadow

lagoon (sounds like la-**goon**): a noun, a body of water

agile (sounds like **a**-jill): an adjective, to move quickly and easily

pronounced (sounds like pro-**nown**-st): an adjective, a very obvious trait

talons (sounds like **tail**-uhn): a noun, claws found on large birds

breach (sounds like **breech**): a verb, to break or violate

impertinent (sounds like im-**purr**-tin-ent): an adjective, rude, brash

burgundy (sounds like **burg**-an-dee): an adjective, deep red color

If you have the Sir Gallant Castle Kit, go to your Workbook now and complete the next lesson, called Banner 12.

CHAPTER THIRTEEN

War of Words

Sir Francis cancelled class for three weeks. Gallant assumed it was on account of his nasty behavior, but this was not enough to bring a correction in his attitude. One day as he stacked firewood outside the door, he heard his father and mother discussing Sir Francis.

"He often travels as **ambassador** for the Lord High Chancellor of England, Sir Thomas More," William explained to Catherine. "Sir Francis has been entrusted with the tasks that require delicate negotiations. I once heard of a **duke** who refused to transfer his share of the crop to the king and an **earl** who withheld the king's tax. Both were visited by Sir Francis in the same week."

Catherine was surprised that nobles would risk offending the king. "How could Sir Francis correct such insolence?"

"Ahh, you've seen his skill with words," William responded. "He is often sent to the most difficult members of nobility, those no one else dares to oppose—and where other knights would draw blood to settle the dispute, Sir Francis uses words skillfully and returns to the High Chancellor with a successful report. Not only that, he often delivers a gift from his meeting, which the offending nobleman offers in apology to the king."

Gallant was unaffected by the praise, and during Sir Francis' absence, he **brooded** and grew increasingly restless. *All these months, I have been boxed in that storeroom, learning tedious things not fit for knights.* Gallant was cross during the days, and at night he tossed and turned and woke often. After nearly two dozen lessons, he still had not been taught to fight with a sword or to ride a horse while wearing armor. *Why do knights need to learn how to plant vegetables? Or count and measure? I brush his horse and fetch his food. I am nothing more than an ordinary servant!*

Gallant was so preoccupied with feeling insulted that he forgot to say his prayers each day. When he did remember, he was too angry to say them. He intended to take his **grievance** to Sir Francis upon his return from the king's errand. It was a daring decision to challenge an adult in this way, but he had already rationalized his misbehavior: *If I am to be a knight, I must not sulk about an offense. I must confront the offender without delay.* He carefully lined up the arguments in his mind for presentation to Sir Francis.

The boy's change in behavior and attitude didn't go unnoticed. He stopped playing his recorder, and he became short-tempered with Margaret and Timothy. They avoided him most days, not sure what had happened to make their older brother so **callous.** Gallant's mother knew that he had been irritable ever since the turkey incident, but she had waited a week before addressing him, hoping he would work through the problem on his own. He didn't. He behaved better around his father, but that was only because he was trying to avoid being **chastised** for his rudeness. He assumed his mother had intervened to delay any disciplinary action, but he knew she had only postponed the reprimand he richly deserved.

One afternoon, Catherine had to remind Gallant to fill the water bucket they kept at the fire. It was the first time in over a year that she had to prompt him for this chore. He brought the bucket in without an apology and then plucked the hand wash basin off the table to empty the dirty water, knowing he should have done this hours earlier. As he returned to the house, Margaret danced past him, bumping into him. He immediately scolded her. "You nearly knocked me over!" he said gruffly. Margaret started to cry. Catherine kissed her cheek and sent her to check on Timothy. She encouraged Gallant to sit down and discuss his concerns with her.

"I've done everything I was asked," he began, as he banged the pewter bowl down on the table. "And all these months I have waited patiently, just as Father instructed me to do." Gallant made a fist and pounded the table. "Was I not supposed to be trained as a knight? Yet I have learned nothing of the sort. I've not held a sword nor worn a gauntlet, and I was cruelly **taunted** at Thornbury Castle—forced to sit in a room full of armor without so much as touching a helmet!"

Catherine listened patiently and stared at the fist Gallant formed. With a nod, she said simply,

"I believe Sir Francis will want to hear what you have to say. But your father and I expect you to treat your brother and sister with kindness, no matter your concerns."

Two weeks later, Sir Francis arrived to the classroom with documents and wax seals to show to Gallant, but Gallant intended to discuss his complaint without delay. After Sir Francis took his seat, Gallant cleared his throat and stood up.

"Sir Francis, I wish to speak." he said.

Sir Francis stopped unwrapping his lesson materials and held up his hand, indicating Gallant should wait. Then he began class in the usual way: "May the Good Lord bless our efforts and pour His Wisdom upon us as we seek to please Him by our studies." Having officially begun class, Sir Francis motioned for him to speak.

"You offered to teach me to be a knight. Instead, you have groomed me as your servant," Gallant said, surprised to have blurted out such a bold statement to his instructor.

Sir Francis leaned back in his chair and paused a moment before replying. "So then, knights should not serve?" Sir Francis asked.

Gallant hadn't thought of it this way. "Well—" Gallant struggled for words.

"I have shown that a knight must be honorable and generous, well-educated, and able to assist in negotiations. That is service, is it not?" Sir Francis said, challenging Gallant.

"Yes," Gallant conceded, "but that is different than being a servant."

Sir Francis stood, walked to the storeroom window and opened the wooden shutter, gazing out as he spoke. "Is the difference then, the fact that a servant is not paid?"

"Yes," Gallant replied **indignantly**. "A servant completes tasks as ordered, without pay and without regard for his own preferences." Gallant was certain he was making excellent points with Sir Francis. *Surely he will agree with me now.*

Instead, Sir Francis posed a question: "Last year, when I traveled to Cambridge to deliver my nephew safely to boarding school, was I a servant? I was not paid."

Gallant began to see that there was a finer distinction between serving and being a servant than he had originally considered. "You were not a servant because you did something you chose to do, something you enjoyed." Gallant retorted.

"And yet, it was an uncomfortable journey for me," Sir Francis **mused.** "It rained nearly the entire trip, and the water seeped into everything we carried. We barely dried out at an inn before returning to the soggy road again. Do you think I enjoyed this task?"

"You aided a relative, a loved one," Gallant countered. "A servant is ordered to help strangers, those with whom he has no family ties."

Sir Francis smiled. "During my royal errand this past week, I was in a position to assist with the harvest at the estate of the Earl of Huntingdon. He was short on staff to bring the crops to market, and so I offered to assist this earl who, before that visit, was a stranger to me. I was not paid, but I served him joyfully. For the two days I labored in loading his wagons, was I not his servant?"

Complaining about being Sir Francis' servant was becoming more difficult for Gallant. He tried another approach: "Well, a servant's tasks are menial, useless to the servant, except perhaps in building muscle. But in the end, the servant has gained nothing by being a servant. He has only made his master's life easier."

Sir Francis nodded slowly and sat back down, reaching into his satchel and pulling out his treasured book. "Your father was a servant once," he said. "Did you know?"

Gallant had heard something about that. As a young man, William had been lent to work on a farm, to help pay debts owed by the family.

"And when the debt was repaid through your father's labor, he was freed. But did he gain nothing?" Sir Francis asked.

Gallant didn't know how to respond.

Sir Francis continued. "If your father had not been sent to the farm to work, he would never have learned how to till his own land and work with the cycles of nature to sow his seeds and harvest his crops. He would not recognize the pests that favor each of the crops, and he would not know how to drive them off. He would not understand the usefulness of letting a field lie **fallow** for a season. Do you still think he gained nothing?"

Gallant protested. "Sir Francis, I mean to say that I have not learned to wield a sword or ride a steed or do any of the things that knights do." Gallant paused dramatically, and then ended with his most biting criticism. "You, sir, have not kept your word."

Gallant thought he would feel a great sense of satisfaction at having gotten the best of Sir

Francis. Instead, he felt a pit in his stomach. He looked down quickly and returned to his seat, a dreadful regret growing inside him. *I just called him a liar. The greatest insult to a knight! Oh, no, what have I done?*

But Sir Francis did not appear to be offended. Instead, he placed his book on the lectern and flipped through the pages until he found a passage, which he read in Latin and then translated for Gallant: "Qui fidelis est ei. That is: 'He that is faithful in that which is least, is faithful also in that which is greater.'" Sir Francis looked up. "When you worked in the garden, you learned the simple task of weeding. And because you did it well, you conveyed to your parents that you could be trusted with more important tasks, such as helping the men of the town to put out a fire. Must a knight be trustworthy?"

Gallant nodded. "Yes, sir."

Sir Francis turned pages and stopped again, reading a passage quietly to himself: "Unusquisque, prout destinavit in corde suo." He continued, louder, "'Let everyone give as he hath determined in his heart, not with sadness, or of necessity, for God loveth a cheerful giver.'" Sir Francis looked up at Gallant. "When you went to the market, you met the old woman in the woods, through whom you were able to practice charity and generosity. Must a knight be charitable and generous?"

Gallant felt a burning in his face. "Yes, sir."

Sir Francis looked back to his book, and turning to a new page, read again: "'For the rest, brethren, whatsoever things are true, whatsoever modest, whatsoever just, whatsoever holy, what-soever lovely, whatsoever of good fame, if there be any virtue, if any praise of discipline, think on these things.'" Again, Sir Francis looked to Gallant. "As you wrote your letter to your Aunt Miriam, you learned to take note only of good and wholesome news. You found the value of your words could bring encouragement and joy. Must a knight speak only in this manner?"

Gallant could only nod.

A few more pages were turned before Sir Francis stopped at another passage. He read, "'Estote ergo vos perfecti sicut et Pater vester caelestis perfectus est. Be you therefore perfect, as also your heavenly Father is perfect.'" Sir Francis held a fist out toward Gallant and spoke forcefully. "The strength of a knight is learned in patient study."

Sir Francis then opened one finger at a time as he drew his conclusion: Lifting his index finger, Sir Francis said, "By pushing your body to run beyond its limits, you learned to overcome the weakness of the flesh." With his middle finger, he added, "By traveling to market, you practiced your capacity to memorize and to follow detailed instructions." With his ring finger: "By studying maps and weights and measures, you learned to engage in **commerce**." And raising his little finger, Sir Francis said: "By embracing kindness for people and animals in a variety of circumstances, you honed the skill of anticipating the needs of others."

With all his fingers extended and his palm facing up, Sir Francis demonstrated that what had been a fist was now a hand extended, as though to help. "The greatest are those who serve the least," he finished.

Sir Francis closed the book. "Do you see, Gallant? By learning to be a servant, you have learned to be a knight. And all this was done in the context of the Holy Scriptures—the Bible, which is our guide to a virtuous life." Sir Francis lifted the book and kissed the cover, then set it gently back on the lectern. "You've learned more about being a knight than you realize." Sir Francis raised his eyebrows and with a kind smile, he said, "So you see, I have done exactly what I promised to do."

Gallant's throat was tight and dry. He now understood what an incredible education he had received from the wise knight who stood before him.

Sir Francis walked nearer to Gallant. "Four hundred years before Jesus, a Greek philosopher named **Socrates** taught a method of learning that we practiced today, though you did not know it. As you presented your arguments, I countered with my own, asking questions to draw out your position. You were forced to hear me and adjust your thinking. Eventually, your position collapsed when you realized it could not be supported by reason and **logic.** A true knight can often avoid a fight through his careful use of words. It may mean a life is spared that day."

Sir Francis sat on the edge of the table. "My young friend, even your complaint was an opportunity for you to learn. Tell me, when did you first feel the discontent? I suspect there was a flash of anger and then a flood of memories that were somehow turned into insult. Do you recall the moment?"

Gallant looked up at Sir Francis with amazement. "Yes. Just after I brushed Donato, when you sent me home. I was angry because I didn't get to ride a knight's horse. Now that I think about it, it was odd. My face felt hot and then all my lessons came to mind, but only to show the ways I had been cheated out of a knight's training. How did you know?"

"You must never forget that a battle rages just out of our sight." Sir Francis comforted Gallant. "Paul wrote to the Ephesians: 'For our wrestling is not against flesh and blood; but against principalities and powers, against the rulers of the world of this darkness, against the spirits of wickedness in the high places.' What you experienced, lad, was an attack by the evil one. The first letter of St. Peter tells us: 'Your adversary the devil, as a roaring lion, goeth about seeking whom he may devour.' He picked a moment when you were most vulnerable and brought to your mind events that could be twisted to support his tainted view. The evil one knew that if he could make you feel offended, it was likely to develop into anger, jealousy, and resentment. He set you up, Master Gallant, because you didn't recognize his trick. Now that you know, do you reject his evil ways?"

"I do reject them," the young boy said firmly.

"Good lad! The next time it happens, immediately call on the Name of the Lord. Praise Him out loud. It will send those beasts scurrying back to hell." Sir Francis swung an open hand in the air to emphasize his point.

Gallant started to feel the same dizziness he experienced the first day he met Sir Francis in the field, when he had challenged Sir Francis with a tree branch. A few more seconds passed as Gallant wiped away tears of embarrassment.

"I beg your forgiveness, sir. I was wrong. I neglected to see the value of this education, and I am no longer worthy of your time." Gallant stood up. "I will tell my father that I have acted improperly and do not deserve further instruction." Shamed, he turned to leave.

Sir Francis stopped him. "Gallant, discouragement is often just another tool of the enemy, to slow us just as we are making progress. Do not **succumb** to it, but press on. I accept your apology. You are closer than you think to your goal, so be of good cheer, my lad. Now, take your seat. We have much to discuss about drawing up legal documents."

Gallant marveled at the patience of Sir Francis. "You're not angry with me?"

"Holding a grudge only serves the enemy." Sir Francis responded definitively. "The Lord Himself has commanded us to forgive 'seventy times seven times.'"

Could I ever be that gracious and forgiving? Gallant sat down as his teacher returned to his lectern and began to unpack documents that had been stamped with wax seals. When Gallant saw a large gold ring Sir Francis used to set his seals, he knew the time had come to resolve the one remaining issue that weighed heavily on him.

Think About This

1. How can you find value in even the smallest chore?

2. Do you see how asking for forgiveness immediately after an offense is much easier than waiting hours or days or weeks?

ambassador (sounds like am-**bass**-uh-door): a noun, a person who acts on behalf of another person or country, often bringing resolution to a conflict

dukes and **earls** (sounds like **dooks** and **erls**): nouns, titles of nobility, persons related to royalty or appointed by royalty

brooded (sounds like **broo**-dead): a verb, moody, sullen,

grievance (sounds like **greeve**-ants): a noun, a complaint lodged against another person

sulk (sounds like **sulk**): a verb, to pout

callous (sounds like **kail**-uhs): an adjective, insensitive, rough

chastised (sounds like chass-**tized**): a verb, to be corrected or sharply disciplined

taunted (sounds like **tawn**-ted): a verb, to tease

indignantly (sounds like inn-**dig**-nant-lee): an adverb, to respond as though greatly offended

mused (sounds like **mews**-d): a verb, to consider thoughtfully, to ponder

fallow (sounds like **fah**-low): an adjective, to plow but not plant anything, to rest the soil

commerce (sounds like **kom**-mirs): a noun, the exchange of goods and services

Socrates (sounds like **sock**-ra-tees): a noun, the proper name of an ancient Greek philosopher

logic (sounds like **lah**-jik): a noun, a thoughtful examination of an issue, using valid arguments

succumb (sounds like suh-**kuhm**): a verb, to give up or surrender

---

If you have the Sir Gallant Castle Kit, go to your Workbook now and complete the next lesson, called Banner 13.

CHAPTER FOURTEEN
Ride to Redemption

Only three days remained before Gallant's final lesson. The dark cloud that had been hanging over him, urging him to be dissatisfied with his training, was gone. Gallant chopped extra wood for the woodpile and cleaned the vegetables he brought from the garden, chores ordinarily done by his father and mother. He invented a new stone game to play with Timothy and he taught rhymes to Margaret whenever she asked.

But there was still one thing that needed to be set right. Gallant had to find a way to return the item he had taken. Time was running out. He decided he needed to fix this problem before his classes ended. It was what a knight would do.

"I'm going out to stable Noctu, Mother!" Gallant did his best thinking when he was around their horse. As he brushed Noctu, his mind drifted back to that fateful day, over a year ago. He and his father had brought their load of wool into Bristol and were on their way to the merchant's row when they observed the commotion around a home just off the town square. They learned that the woman's husband had died, and she had to move to a distant village to live with a relative.

As they rode past the house, Gallant saw several women hugging and crying quietly near the door as the men loaded the woman's furniture, bundles of clothing and sacks of food onto a waiting wagon. The light tan-skinned horse hitched to the wagon looked out of place, large and stocky and too majestic to be pulling a wagon at all. Gallant shrugged and turned his attention back to their task. His father used to ride Noctu with the wool sacks tied to his saddle; but now that Gallant was older, William tossed the large bundles of wool into the wagon and hitched Noctu so Gallant could come along. Once they reached the market, William relied on Gallant to help him find the best price for their wool. They would split up and quiz the vendors before meeting back at Noctu to compare their information.

After their business transaction was completed, William stayed in the market to discuss the latest news with the other men and Gallant wandered around town. When he passed the widow's home, the wagon was gone, the door was closed, and the visitors had all dispersed. Gallant noticed the glint of sunlight flashing from an object on the ground near the spot where the wagon had stood. He ran to see what caused the glimmer and found a ring lying in the dirt. With a rush of exhilaration, he reached for it and quickly stuffed it in his jacket. *Finders keepers!* He planned to examine it more closely when he wouldn't be seen.

As Gallant returned to their wagon to wait for his father, he felt a twinge in his heart. *Why did you hurry to hide the ring from view? Shouldn't you tell your Father what you found?* He stopped and looked quickly all around him. The street was unusually quiet and still. Another thought came to him. *It's nothing. Don't worry, no one saw you. And the ring is yours.*

"Yes. It's mine. I found it." Gallant pushed the guilty feeling out of his mind. When William arrived at the wagon to take them home, the boy said nothing about the ring.

Later that evening, while he was feeding the sheep, he pulled the ring out of his jacket and looked at it closely. The chunky gold **signet** ring was about the same size as the one Sir Francis had brought to the writing lesson, but it had a lamb in the center, with Latin words around the rim. *Via Veritas Vita. I wonder what that means.* Gallant knew this kind of ring was used to confirm the owner's identity in the sale or exchange of goods.

During his class about signet rings and wax seals, Sir Francis had given Gallant a short, round tin and instructed him to fetch a large ember from the fire in his home. When he returned with the ember, Gallant watched as his teacher used short forceps to hold the ember over a small piece of red-colored beeswax. The chunk melted into a coin-sized molten puddle. Sir Francis slid his signet ring on, just past the first knuckle of his index finger, and pushed the ring into the soft wax, leaving behind the design of the ring. It was a formal script "F" with scrolls and vines around it, similar to the one Sir Francis had drawn the day Gallant learned to use the quill.

"The seal acts as proof of the identity of a particular man or the authority of a specific office," Sir Francis had explained. "A king will use his seal to authenticate a gift of land to a baron. A court will use their seal when they rule on a dispute between neighboring dukes."

Gallant was convinced the gold ring he found was worth a great deal, but no legitimate merchant would pay a farm boy for a ring that clearly belonged to nobility. He wrapped it in a piece of scrap deerskin and buried it in the woods in a place only he would know.

The hidden ring burned in Gallant's heart like a smoldering coal. Learning the ways of a true knight set the coal ablaze. For months, Gallant had been planning how to correct his terrible decision. *It's not enough to simply tell Mother and Father and Sir Francis about my poor judgment. I must make amends first. I will find the widow and return the ring. I shall confess my misdeed afterwards.* Gallant's plan meant that he had to discover where she had moved and then find a way to get there, all without disobeying his parents or his tutor, or leaving the farm without permission. Gallant dug up the ring, placed it in his money bag, and waited for his chance.

Soon afterwards, an opportunity presented itself. William decided Gallant was ready to travel alone to bring the second shearing of wool to the market. His father strapped two sacks of fleece across Noctu's back end.

"The sacks are not heavy, but they are awkward, Gallant," his father said. "Once you get to market, untie the leather strap and let them fall to the ground. Noctu is used to carrying these loads and having them dropped at his feet. Take the time you need to bargain with the buyers and find the best price. You've been with me often enough." William put his hand on his son's shoulder and added, "Stay away from that villain with the missing finger—you know the one. His scale is never accurate. And remember, Noctu is a good horse, but he is still just a horse. He will go where he is led. Tie him when you arrive at market and keep an eye on him as you visit the buyers."

Gallant nodded. He was eager to be on his way.

Catherine packed a hearty lunch for him and tied the canvas food bag and a water flask to the saddle. She kissed his forehead. "You've grown up," she said with a tear in her eye. "I knew the day would come."

"I'll be back before nightfall, Mother," Gallant promised cheerfully. No one knew about his secret mission now, but he was eager to tell them all about it when he returned. William gave Gallant a foot lift and he climbed aboard Noctu. "Until evening!" he said, and the horse trotted away.

The ride into town was the best Gallant could recall, because he knew he was about to fix something that had bothered him for many long months. He wondered how the widow would react. *It doesn't matter, whether good or ill. The ring must be returned to its rightful owner.* Gallant arrived in town and carried the wool sacks from **vendor** to vendor. After quizzing them all, he established the best price and sold the fleece, dropping twelve **shillings** into his money bag.

Gallant brought Noctu to a village field where he could graze, while the boy sat on the grass near his horse and hurried to eat his own lunch. Following the meal, he led Noctu to a trough for water while he reached for the flask his mother had sent along. When they both had quenched their thirst, Gallant gathered the reins and walked with Noctu to the house where the widow once lived. It was a prominent home near the main square, set on large swath of property. He knocked and waited. In time, a woman pulled open the heavy wooden door, wiping her hands on her apron. Gallant bowed respectfully.

"God save you. I'm looking for the widow who used to live here. Can you direct me to her?" Gallant asked.

The woman looked past the boy and saw Noctu standing a few paces away. "God save you. It's good you have a mount," she said. "She moved eighty furlongs from here, to a village called Bath. Southeast. You can follow the main road out of town. It leads to the center square of Bath."

Gallant bowed again and turned to leave, then remembered he needed more information. "Who is she? Who do I ask for when I reach Bath?"

The woman seemed surprised by the question. "Why, she is Lady Bennett, widow of Sir Bennett, a knight of the Duke of Buckingham," the woman said, adding, "Sir Bennett died nobly, defending a traveling merchant who was being robbed by scoundrels."

A knight! Of course, I should have known when I saw his horse that day. But oh, did he have to be in the service of that Duke? Gallant had visited Thornbury Castle not long ago. *How embarrassing to think that Lady Grace will hear of my breach of virtue. Well, it can't be helped.* Gallant thanked the woman and stroked Noctu's nose. "We must ride swiftly my friend, if we are to return home by nightfall."

Gallant pulled himself atop his horse and headed out of town. The journey took about an hour and a half, with Noctu alternating between a full trot and a canter. Gallant arrived in a village much like his own and called to a passerby, "Pardon me, sir. Can you tell me where to find Lady Bennett?"

The man pointed to a home built on top of a small crest. "She'll likely be sewing when you find her. She's the finest seamstress in the Kingdom."

Gallant nodded his thanks and headed toward the home. When he arrived, he dropped down off Noctu and tied his reins to a fence near the entry. He took a deep breath, smoothed his clothing, and knocked. The door was opened by a manservant.

"I have come to deliver an item of importance to Lady Bennett," he said boldly. Gallant was led around to a back garden, where an attractive middle-aged woman wearing a blue silk dress was sitting on a stool under the shade of a tree. She was embroidering a fancy cross in red thread onto a square white cloth. The servant leaned close to her ear and whispered. She stopped her work and watched Gallant approach, but said nothing.

Gallant bowed low. "God save you, my Lady Bennett. I am Gallant of Bristol, son of William. I come to make amends for the terrible manner in which I have wronged you." His voice was quivering.

Lady Bennett set her project on a table next to her and dismissed the servant with a wave of her hand. After he departed, she looked intently at the boy before her. "Young Gallant," she replied, "I do not know you. How is it that you have wronged me?"

Gallant reached into his money bag and pulled out the signet ring. He looked at it one last time, shook his head in shame and carried it to Lady Bennett. When she saw the ring, tears filled her eyes. She took the ring gingerly and held it to her heart, her eyes closed, tears streaming. Gallant continued speaking. "I found it on the ground in front of your home after you departed Bristol. I knew it belonged to you, and yet I dared to keep it hidden all these months. Someday I hope to pay you for the time you lived without such a treasure. For now, I can only beg your forgiveness."

Lady Bennett kissed the ring and spoke as she wept. "It was my...my husband's ring. When I did not find it among his things, I assumed the bandits who killed him had taken it. It must have been in a jacket pocket, or caught up in the fabric of his breeches as the clothing was carried to the cart." Lady Bennett paused a moment as the tears continued to flow. She slowly blinked them away and looked at Gallant. "I could have used it to transfer property and buy what I needed. Being without it has been a grave hardship."

Gallant was ashamed that he had caused such difficulty for a widow. He knelt on one knee before Lady Bennett, took her hand, and held it tenderly. "These past few months, the wise and learned Sir Francis has instructed me in the ways of a knight. Now I understand what a vile action it was to keep that precious ring. I can only tell you that I shall never conduct myself in this way again. Can you forgive me, my lady?"

Lady Bennett slowly removed her hand from his and stood, turning away as she wiped her eyes. Gallant rose to his feet and took a step backward, pausing respectfully to await her reply. Every sound around Gallant was amplified. Crows cackled in the branches above.

In the distance, Noctu snorted and whinnied. Crickets chirped and the trees rustled with an intermittent breeze. It seemed to him that he had been standing there for half the day, though it was really only a part of a minute before Lady Bennett turned back to Gallant and spoke with clear determination.

"Gallant. I forgive you. You see, I, too, made a poor decision in my youth, one summer day, a lifetime ago." Lady Bennett paused, then admitted, "I never corrected it and now it is too late to do so. The person I wronged is dead. I carry the weight of being unable to make **recompense**. I will not cause such a burden to another."

Gallant bowed low. "I mean to repay you for your grief. Give me but a few years to gather together some coins."

"That will not be necessary," Lady Bennett responded.

"Then, allow me to serve you in your field— or, or task me with errands," he protested.

"No, Gallant. For many years I set aside my needlework. I declined even the requests of the Bishop while Sir Bennett lived; so comfortable was I, enjoying my husband's good fortune and the renown of his name. The Lord has shown me that the use of my skill pleases Him and that this labor is to God's glory. I have benefited from the trial."

Lady Bennett paused a moment and turned the ring over in her hand, gazing at it lovingly. "I, too, know Sir Francis. His wisdom in settling disputes is far beyond his years. He once reminded my husband that all things work together for good, for those who love God and work according to His purpose." She looked at Gallant.

"Sir Francis had come to warn us about an attempt by our enemies to take my husband by force, exacting a substantial payment for his return. It was a frightful message. My husband later told me—" Lady Bennett stopped mid-sentence. She looked at the ring with a stunned surprise, mouthing silent words.

Then she spoke with astonishment, staring off in the distance. "Why, today is the feast of St. George, my husband's patron saint! My husband told me that if ever he were in captivity, he would send his ring as a token, the moment he was released; and that he would ask St. George to escort it safely back to me." Lady Bennett looked at Gallant with wide eyes. "It is no coincidence you arrived this day."

Lady Bennett suddenly dropped onto her knees on the grass and crossed her hands over her heart, looking up to the sky. "Te Deum laudamus! Thank you, my Lord God, for receiving his soul. I praise You for your abundant mercy in allowing this message to come to me." She remained in silent prayer a moment and then stirred, ready to stand.

Quickly, Gallant stepped forward and extended his hand to Lady Bennett. With a warm smile, she took the young boy's hand and stood, wiping the last tears from her eyes. Gallant noticed her mournful expression had turned to immense joy. She released his hand and held the ring close to her heart. "Be on your way, young knight. You have repaid your debt by returning the ring. And you have brought me greater comfort than you will ever know. I bid you greet Sir Francis on my behalf when next you see him."

Lady Bennett raised her hand in farewell. "Godspeed your journey home."

It was a new Gallant who jumped aboard Noctu. *She called me a knight. I have done what a knight must do.* He could not have imagined the joy he would feel once this issue was resolved. He said a prayer of thanksgiving to God for having graciously allowed such a pleasant resolution to a problem that had **vexed** him for months —a problem he himself had created. *God is so good. His mercy endures forever!* He tapped Noctu on his flank to spur him on, and he headed home at a gallop, slowing occasionally to give his horse a rest.

Gallant arrived back at his family farm by dusk. He brushed and stabled Noctu, then called a greeting as he pulled open the house door. His mother stepped to the fire to scoop his supper from the pan, but Gallant insisted she sit with his father at the table.

First, he produced the coins from the sale of the fleece. "Now I must speak about a matter of utmost urgency," he began. "Mother. Father. What I tell you will **grieve** you, but I hope I have done what is necessary to restore your confidence in me."

And so Gallant told his tale of failure and redemption; of evil and good. It was, in fact, a tale about how a farm boy learned to be a knight. And that evening, for the first time in many months, Gallant slept soundly.

Think About This

1. Can you think of any wrong you would like to fix?

2. Some wrongs cannot be corrected easily. Wouldn't it be better not to commit them at all, rather than to try to fix them later?

Word Helper

redemption (sounds like ree-**dem**-shun): a noun, being saved from sin or evil

signet (sounds like **sig**-net): a noun, a ring with designs or initials carved into the main surface

fleece (sounds like **flees**): a noun, the wool covering a sheep

villain (sounds like **vill**-an): a noun, a criminal or a person who does bad things

vendor (sounds like **ven**-door): a noun, a person who buys or sells products

shilling (sounds like **shill**-ing): a noun, a silver coin worth 1/20 of a sovereign gold coin

recompense (sounds like **reck**-come-pents): a verb, to correct damage, to make amends

vexed (sounds like **vecks**-d): an adjective, to be upset or irritated

grieve (sounds like **greeve**): a verb, to cause distress or pain

If you have the Sir Gallant Castle Kit, go to your Workbook now and complete the next lesson, called Banner 14.

CHAPTER FIFTEEN
Commencement

Gallant awoke to the sounds of his father collecting the buckets to milk the goats. He jumped out of bed. "Father, shall I skim the cream?"

William chuckled. Gallant could tell that his father knew why he was so eager to help. "Draw a fresh bucket of water from the well instead," he said, shaking his head. "Your mother will handle the skimming, as she always does."

Gallant dressed quickly and rushed to complete his chores. Today was his final day of class. Part of him wished he could hurry the day along, because it meant he was closer to being a knight. Part of him was saddened his time with Sir Francis was at an end. Gallant brought the water, then cleaned the stable and set out fresh hay for Noctu; returning in time to share a breakfast of bread and eggs with his family.

"This is to be Gallant's last day of school," his mother announced as they all sat at table. Timothy and Margaret cheered with great enthusiasm.

"Hooray!! Hooray for Gallant!" the two young ones cried out.

It sounded like a reason to celebrate, but Gallant was **reticent** to do so. *Sir Francis has been more than my tutor. He is a reminder of what I can be.* William put his arm around Gallant's shoulders as he sat next to him.

"I've heard good reports from Sir Francis," William said proudly. "He tells me that the only thing that delays your knighting is your size."

It would not have made sense to try to learn to swing a sword if I could not hold it on my own. Now I understand why all the other lessons must be learned before a weapon is ever held. "I will miss my training, Father," Gallant said.

"Well, this is a joyous occasion," Catherine reminded everyone. "We mustn't turn it into a day of sadness. Come and see Sir Francis' payment." She approached their wooden chest and pulled out a beautiful blue woolen blanket. "I finished the weaving just yesterday." The blanket, which was large enough to cover a sleeping man, had been woven with wool thread dyed with finely ground **azurite,** a blue mineral.

Gallant gasped. "Mother! It's so beautiful. This belongs in the Thornbury Castle, covering the Duke himself!"

"It's stunning, my love!" William exclaimed as he examined the woven piece closely.

Timothy and Margaret rushed to touch the blanket. Margaret took a corner and spun around to wrap herself tightly in the warm covering.

William laughed. "You may have trouble separating her from such a lovely piece!"

Catherine was pleased with their praise. "Oh, my! You all tempt me to the sin of pride," she said with a fluttering laugh. "I give God the glory. Now, enough of the flattery, let's welcome the gift of this day. There is much to be done before sunset."

William checked the contents of his bag and added the lunch his wife had made. "I'll be trimming the fruit trees and repairing the fences, but

I look forward to seeing you all at supper. My dear Catherine, do convince Sir Francis to stay for a meal."

Gallant's mother nodded and grasped her husband's hand as they parted.

Gallant picked up his chalk and slate, his quill pen, and a wrapped package about as long as his forearm and as wide as a few fingers. Gallant had traded some fleece scraps his father gave him for a piece of linen at the market a week earlier. The package he held was wrapped in that linen and tied with a woolen string. He bowed to his mother and waved to the little ones before he headed out the door to the storeroom.

As he walked, he thought about how blessed he had been to receive the training from Sir Francis. He stopped and called to mind the prayer he and his father often said as William sheared the sheep.

"How shall I render account to the Lord for all the good He has done for me? I will take up the cup of salvation and call upon the Lord. Praising, I will call His Name and I will be saved from my enemies." Gallant nodded to himself, pleased to have said such a fitting prayer.

When he arrived in his schoolroom, he sat at his desk and arranged his items neatly before him. Within a few minutes, he heard the now familiar clop-clop of Donato's hooves and the creaking of the saddle as Sir Francis dismounted. As usual, his teacher entered the storeroom and hung his hat while Gallant stood and bowed to greet him.

"Good morning, sir."

"Good morning, Master Gallant."

Sir Francis gestured to Gallant. "Please begin class with our prayer," he said.

Gallant recited the prayer, though he had never said it out loud before. "May the good Lord bless our efforts and pour His Wisdom upon us as we seek to please Him by our studies." *Wow! How did I do that?*

Sir Francis didn't appear to be surprised. Gallant remained standing and spoke with a confident boldness. "Sir Francis, before we begin class, I beg you allow me to confess a misdeed from my past."

Sir Francis nodded. And so Gallant explained the story of the ring, how he took it, kept it, and returned it. He told Sir Francis how he offered to make amends, and he related how gracious Lady Bennett responded. He did not, however, tell Sir Francis that she had admitted to making an error in earlier days. Gallant had learned never to pass gossip or speak unkindly about another person, even when the story was true. Lastly, Gallant passed along Lady Bennett's greeting. When he finished his tale, Gallant waited breathlessly for Sir Francis' reaction.

"I approve of the manner in which you corrected your mistake," he said simply. "Please be seated, Gallant." With that, Sir Francis began the class. "So, we have come to our last day of lessons. Do you understand the significance of a coat-of-arms?"

Gallant nodded affirmatively. "It is a part of the **heraldry** of a family, a record of their honor and a symbol of their most treasured attributes."

Sir Francis placed his satchel on the table in front of Gallant. "Yes, and it is often a reflection of the accomplishments of the family line. Have you ever considered what you would choose to **memorialize** in your family's coat-of-arms if you had the opportunity?"

Gallant was astonished at the question. "Oh, no, sir. Only those of nobility are worthy of this honor."

Sir Francis responded with gentle, but firm authority. "Nobility comes from the heart, not the money bag, Gallant." He opened his satchel and pulled out several pages filled with colorful drawings of coat-of-arms, some which Gallant recognized. One was the Duke of Buckingham's. Others he had seen at a fair, but many were unknown to him.

Sir Francis spread the pages on the desk in front of Gallant. "Study the images, Gallant." Sir Francis instructed. "These will help you consider what to include in your coat-of-arms. Whenever possible, look to the work of those who have gone before you and build upon it. There will always be someone who is better than you— in this endeavor: a more creative artist, or a better illustrator. Do not compare your talent to theirs. Rather, reap the benefit from their example and then create something you can claim as your own."

Gallant looked at each design and slowly moved his gaze from one to the other. He recognized the falcon image in one and a prancing deer in another. He saw swords and arrows, helmets and crowns. He recognized foxes, pelicans, bears, rearing horses, and winged lions. There was a significant variety of colors and shapes as well. Stripes and solids, wavy and straight lines were incorporated into the designs. Each was a fascinating study on the history of a family, and Gallant was captivated by the collection of the coat-of-arms before him.

Sir Francis spoke as Gallant continued to study the images. "The color white symbolizes purity. Red is often used to depict sacrifice, perhaps a bloody death for a righteous cause. Purple is reserved for those of royal heritage and black usually represents a sturdy resistance; for example, fighting against a king who ruled as a **tyrant**."

"Blue." Gallant interrupted, "What is the symbolism behind the color blue?"

Sir Francis smiled and answered, "A good choice, my lad. It stands for truth and loyalty and strength. What symbols would you include?"

Gallant did not hesitate. He had been picturing the symbols in his mind as he moved from picture to picture. "Sheep," Gallant said confidently, "because by this our family is known in Bristol. And a plow, because of the work of my father in the field, learned as a young boy in servitude." Sir Francis nodded approvingly.

"I should want to include the sword which you generously donated to our family. It represents the introduction of knighthood into our family line. I am most grateful for this opportunity, for me and for those who come after." Gallant looked at Sir Francis and then he glanced at the Bible resting on the table. "I intend to include a large cross on the coat-of-arms. Mother reminds us that we would have nothing were it not for the goodness of the Lord God. Father would have us know our faith as well as any topic, perhaps better."

Sir Francis pulled another sheet from his satchel, a blank page of his personal paper. "Excellent. Draw your coat-of-arms here, Gallant" he said, "and as my parting gift, I shall have it painted on canvas. My father will petition the King for its submission to the Royal Herald of Arms for registry."

Gallant was so overcome by the offer that he could think of nothing to say. He stood and bowed low, as his best expression of gratitude. He then picked up the package wrapped in linen and carried it to Sir Francis. "Never could I equal your favors to my family and to me, Sir Francis, but I mean to share my most treasured gift, to thank you." He handed Sir Francis the package and watched as Sir Francis untied the string and unwrapped the linen fabric. It was the wooden recorder, given to Gallant by James in Thornbury.

Sir Francis had often heard Gallant playing the recorder before and after class and he knew that he had become proficient. This was a heartfelt gift, one that Gallant could not replace, and Sir Francis accepted it graciously. "Thank you. It is most generous of you."

Gallant returned to his seat and began work on his family's coat-of-arms. He spent an hour designing the shield and another hour adding color pigment. His teacher provided a variety of colors in small containers filled with ground stone and crushed flowers. He showed Gallant how to mix colors to create additional tints. Gallant rubbed the stone and flower mixtures into the paper with his finger until he was satisfied with the colors. All the while, Sir Francis was content to sit at the table and read his Bible. When Gallant finished, he held up the design for Sir Francis.

"Well done," Sir Francis responded. "There is one lesson, still, Gallant. It is perhaps the most important you shall learn." Sir Francis carried his Bible to the lectern. "No matter your successes, never claim them as your own. You have received many precious gifts." Sir Francis turned several pages and found a passage, which he quoted. "Holy Scripture tells us, 'And unto whomsoever much is given, of him much shall be required.' Your obligation is greater than the obligations of others who have been less gifted. Never stop striving to *be* your best, to *do* your best. And when you accomplish much and are highly praised, do not take the praise to yourself, but turn it to God, who is the Giver. Remember that your gifts were given to you so that you could serve others. Do you understand?"

Gallant nodded solemnly.

"That was the lesson on the first day of school, when you arrived after class had begun. It is the quickest and the surest way to knighthood." Sir Francis paused a moment, lost in thought. "You are on the path, Gallant. Do not stray to the left or to the right and you will achieve your goal of knighthood."

"Yes, sir."

"Enough for the day." Sir Francis announced. He packed his satchel for the last time, and the two walked in silence toward Gallant's home. The scent of baking bread reached them before they arrived at the door. On the days Gallant had been at class, William had worked to construct a stone and clay oven for Catherine outdoors, just beyond the house entrance. It meant that she would have the entire fire pit inside the home for the meat and vegetable pots. Today, the bread smelled wonderful. It was nearly done. When they arrived home, Catherine welcomed them both. "God save you, Sir Francis, and you, my young Gallant."

"God save you," they replied in unison.

Catherine excused herself. "Sir Francis, please, have a seat inside while I retrieve the loaf. William and I would have you join us for a meal before you depart. He should be home shortly." Sir Francis paused at the door, then turned and took a step to the woodpile. He sat down on a stack of wood, nearly a stool's height.

"Allow me to enjoy the sun's light until William returns," Sir Francis responded.

Catherine nodded and retrieved the loaf from the oven, bunching her apron at the corners to carry the bread without burning her hands. When she had placed it inside on the table, Gallant asked her quietly: "Why does Sir Francis not join us inside?"

Catherine smiled thoughtfully. "Sir Francis is a gentleman. And no gentleman would be alone with another man's wife; even under the most innocent circumstances." Catherine continued to set the table for supper, as Gallant gathered the little ones to help them wash.

About a quarter hour passed before William was heard greeting Sir Francis outside. Catherine rushed to the door, brushing cheeks with William as he entered.

"Well, you did it, my old friend," William was saying to Sir Francis as they both set down their bags, "just as you said. You have taught my son to be a knight."

"He is not a knight yet," Sir Francis corrected him. "Still he needs training in the art of battle. But that requires greater size and strength, and Gallant will grow into that soon enough."

William waited until Sir Francis and Gallant had washed in the basin, then he splashed his face and arms and dried them with a cloth. When all were prepared, they sat at the trestle table together with Margaret and Timothy while Catherine served them a delightful feast of roasted lamb, turnips with herbs and thick slices of the wheat bread, topped with apple jam made from their fruit trees. William said the blessing and poured wine in goblets for the adults. For the first time, he poured a short glass for Gallant. Though he had tasted wine before, this was the first time Gallant was given his own serving. He understood it meant he was now a responsible young man.

William spoke with Sir Francis about the news of the town, the market prices for fleece and crops, and the latest **edicts** from the king. When dinner was finished, Catherine cleared the table of the dishes and waited for a break in the conversation. When it came, she announced: "Sir Francis, we have your payment." She pulled the blue wool blanket from the trunk and presented it to Sir Francis. Margaret didn't realize it was a gift, so she quickly ran to the blanket, grabbed a fistful of fabric and held it close to her cheek.

Sir Francis examined the fabric carefully and gingerly took Catherine's hand and kissed it. "I will treasure this as long as I live," he said. "It is a masterpiece of color and a demonstration of great skill at the loom. Thank you, my Lady Catherine." A quiet moment passed while Catherine gently separated Margaret from the blanket, holding her close so she would not complain.

"Well," Sir Francis announced, "the time has come for my departure. Gallant, you turned ten during the time of your lessons, did you not?"

"Yes, sir." Gallant replied. Sir Francis continued: "I have spoken with your father. On your fourteenth birthday, I will return to take you to the court of the Earl of Rutland, in his grand estate in North East Leicestershire. There you will work as a squire to Sir Edmund, a knight distinguished in bravery and wisdom. And you will benefit greatly from serving during the construction of the Earl's castle."

Gallant was overjoyed to hear that his lessons would continue, but he turned with concern to his father. "But what of my chores? The farm and the sheep?" Gallant knew how much his father relied on his help.

William pointed to his younger son. "By that time, Timothy will be old enough to assume your duties and Margaret will assist your mother with the cooking and the weaving. We will manage."

Catherine interrupted: "Though we shall miss you sorely, dear one."

"There is one final issue which must be addressed," Sir Francis said sternly. "Gallant, you should know that you will not be the first knight in your family line."

Gallant looked quickly to Sir Francis, stunned by the news. *Not the first knight? Who else then?*

Sir Francis walked over to Gallant's father and spoke with a formal bearing. "Sir William, allow me to present Gallant, my student and a student of knighthood." And to Gallant, he said: "Gallant, I present Sir William, Baron of Bristol."

My father is a knight? And the Baron of Bristol? Gallant looked with surprise at his father, saw his smiling mother at his side, and gasped: "How? How can that be?"

Sir Francis took a moment to explain. "You see, when we were both young men, your father saved me from certain death."

Gallant's mouth dropped open. *This must be what they spoke of, that first night as they talked late into the night.*

"William came upon me while I was under attack by a villain who had a dispute with a baron under my father's authority. The scoundrel could not gain access to the baron or my father, so he laid in wait for me. I was taken by surprise, coming home from an afternoon of bartering and laden down with deer skins. Your father tackled the rogue—a man twice his size—seconds before he would have pierced me through with his sword. We held him there in the field, until our cries for help were answered by concerned passersby. In gratitude, my father issued a battlefield knighting. He granted four hundred acres and sixty sheep to your father, payable when he should reach the age of twenty-one. By the time your father turned twenty, he was married and had already established a small farm just outside Bristol. He declined to accept any property as payment, but agreed to receive the title, Sir William, Baron of Bristol Manor. In humility, your father has kept news of the title to himself all these years. Only your mother knew."

Sir Francis bowed deeply to William and said: "My father sends his warmest regards, Sir William, and bids you join him at the castle at your convenience, to discuss Gallant's **apprenticeship.**"

Sir William and Sir Francis embraced. After a smile and a nod, Sir Francis headed to the door. Just before he reached it, he turned and pulled two pieces of candied ginger from his satchel and handed them to Margaret and Timothy. "A consolation, because you bore the absence of your dear brother for all the long summer," he said to the children. Margaret took her piece eagerly. It was barely in her hand before she licked it. Timothy took the candy from Sir Francis' outstretched hand

and stared at it, his brow furrowed with thought. He dug in his pocket and pulled out the ginger Sir Francis had given him months earlier. It was covered with dirt and lint from his pocket.

"Well done!" Sir Francis laughed. "You've already mastered the art of delaying simple pleasures." Timothy wasn't sure what Sir Francis meant, but he was delighted to have two pieces of ginger candy. He grinned, brushed off the old piece and popped it in his mouth, placing the new ginger piece into his pocket.

Gallant remembered Sir Francis' initial visit to the house, when he had first given candied ginger to the two young ones. *I thought he didn't give me any because he saw the dark secret I held in my heart. I considered it a cruel gesture, a reprimand. Now I understand, he meant the gift as a comfort to my siblings.* Gallant's final lesson had been a critical one and he vowed to abide by the lesson always. *Never again will I judge the actions of another unless it be to give honor or thanks.*

Sir Francis left the home of Sir William and Lady Catherine, Gallant, Margaret, and Timothy. They all followed him outside, dismayed to have to bid farewell to their beloved friend. Margaret sensed the sadness in the others and began to cry, just as Catherine picked her up and held her tight. The knight folded his new blanket and secured it to his saddle, then untied Donato and mounted the steed for his trip home.

"God save you, Sir Francis," Gallant's voice cracked as he called out. He quickly wiped a tear that had formed and bowed deeply to Sir Francis, who tipped his hat as his horse trotted away. After Sir Francis was out of earshot, Gallant turned to William.

"Father, there is something that troubles me."

"Tell me," William replied. They stood together watching Sir Francis disappear into the tree line.

Gallant took a deep breath. "It sometimes seemed as if Sir Francis had no emotion. When I offended him, he did not fume with anger. When he received the beautiful blanket, he did not shout for joy. Does a knight have no feeling?" Gallant's voice quivered with concern. *Perhaps I will be unable to master this challenge and as a result, never reach knighthood.*

William knelt on one knee in front of Gallant, taking him by the shoulders and hugging him tightly. When he released him, William spoke with misty eyes. "Son, a man's emotions are what inflame his compassion for others. You must never lose that. Sir Francis does not disregard his passions, rather he keeps them in their proper place. A mature man understands that when he is moved to the extremes of emotion, his thinking becomes cloudy and he has lost his ability to judge fairly and to act rationally."

Catherine stepped closer and stroked Gallant's cheek. "Son, once you have learned to maintain a steady peace in your heart," she said, "no praise will inflate you and no failure will dishearten you. Whether rich or poor, healthy or ailing; in all circumstances, you will find the serenity of God's will. It is a secret that, sadly, many men never learn. You are blessed to know two men who have not only learned the secret, but mastered it."

William rose and placed his arm around Catherine's waist. He cleared his throat, moved by his wife's sweet words. "Sir Francis and I learned that secret from the Lord, who speaks through the Scriptures," William said, gazing at the trees where he had last seen Sir Francis. "It was St. Paul who said: 'I speak not as it were for want. For I have learned, in whatsoever state I am, to be content therewith.'"

Gallant looked up at his father and mother with great tenderness. "I am most grateful for the instruction of Sir Francis. But I realize that much of what I learned from him, I had already seen at home." Gallant looked around at their property and the fields full of sheep. He saw the house and stable, the storeroom and the crops. He and his siblings were well fed, well clothed and they were taught the importance of a good life. He remembered how his parents always had something for any poor beggar who might cross their path, and he recalled how often they gave thanks to God—even when circumstances were not to their preference. Gallant spoke again.

"I should have known you were a knight, Father; and that you were a lady, Mother. All you have done gives evidence of your generosity and charity. How shall I ever repay you?"

Catherine leaned down and kissed Gallant on the forehead. William responded in a quiet, calm voice: "Live well, son. That is payment enough."

Think About This

1. Can you think of a time you jumped to a conclusion about someone's behavior, and then you found out later you were mistaken? Wouldn't it have been better to assume the best about that person and not the worst?

2. It is hard work to live the way a knight must live. Are you up for the challenge?

Word Helper

reticent (sounds like **ret**-ih-sent): an adverb, to be hesitant

azurite (sounds like **az**-your-ite): a noun, a blue mineral, used in dyes and paints

heraldry (sounds like **hair**-all-dree): a noun, the collection of the coat-of-arms, crest and insignia used on clothing and shields that represent a particular noble lineage

memorialize (sounds like mem-**oar**-ee-all-eyes): a verb, to make permanent

tyrant (sounds like **tie**-rant): a noun, a leader who oppresses the people under his rule